A DUSTY CHRISTMAS

LILLIANA ROSE

ISBN-13: 978-0-6487640-7-6

A DUSTY CHRISTMAS

To my sister, Annette,
keep on farming on.

INFORMATION AND DICTIONARY

This book has been written using US English, but the book's story is set in Australia. Some euphemisms that form part of the Australian spoken word may be used. If you would like further explanation, or to discuss Australia, please do not hesitate to contact the author. Contact details have been provided, for your convenience, at the end of this book.

Akubra – Felt hat traditionally worn by farmers.

Auger – Is used to raise and transport grain from the ground to the top of grain bins, load trucks, or carry feed.

Bloody – A swear word used to emphasize a comment or angry statement.

Boxing Day – Holiday celebrated the day after Christmas Day.

Bush – Refers to sparsely settled areas of Australia, usually scrub-covered or forested wilderness.

Chook – A hen or chicken.

Combine – Refers to the part of the harvester which is in front and has moving blades to cut the stalks of the crop.

Combine Harvester – A versatile machine designed to efficiently harvest a variety of grain crops.

Cuppa – A cup of tea.

Drove me batty – Frustrated to the point of exasperation.

Durum Wheat – Also called pasta wheat or macaroni wheat – it has a very high protein content relative to normal wheat but is low in gluten.

Esky – Portable cooler or icebox.

Fisticuffs – Fighting with the fists.

Hard Yakka – Australian workwear including shoes.

Header – A implement that can be mounted on the front of a harvester enabling it to cut crops or perform other crop-related activities.

Iffy – Full of uncertainty and doubt.

Jubilee cake – A light fruit cake.

Mate – Refers to a friend.

Mob – A group of sheep also known as a flock or herd.

Pub – Hotel.

Rossi – Brand of boots.

Royal Adelaide Show – Annual agricultural show in Adelaide South Australia.

Service Station – Gas filling station.

Smoko – A short break from work.

Take Away – Takeout food.

Ute – A utility vehicle or pick-up truck.

Wanker – A general insult and used as abuse.

Wrangler – Clothing designed in Australia for our unique environment.

CHAPTER 1

Wednesday, December 18th, 2019

Dusty Miller stepped down from the cab of the John Deere combine harvester. Her steel-toe work boots thumped on the grated metal steps, the sound lost in the roar from the engine. Her body stiff from sitting for nearly three hours straight, and her mind tired from concentrating lining up the rotating 'cutting bar' or header, to cut the wheat stalks. It was important not to miss any of the crop.

Fortunately, this year the crop was good, thick and tall, unlike last year where it was short, which meant the header had to be set very low to the ground and was at risk of getting damaged by rocks.

Each stalk's worth money in the bank, and there was a big need to fill the coffers, the crops were after all, a major income for her farm, Acacia Plains, on the Yorke Peninsula. She'd been running the farm for the last three years since her father died of a heart attack.

In a way, it was just another harvest. But this year was a little different. She wasn't single.

Nearly a year ago, hot accountant, Blaise Johns, had come into her life, and it was as if her country life collided with his city life in a humungous bang, leaving them attracted to each other.

This year, while going around and around each paddock, first harvesting the barley, and now the durum wheat, her mind easily became distracted with thoughts of him. And their future.

Had he proved himself as a worthy man to work on the land with her?

Bloody hell, he had so much to learn, and while there was an attraction, a brewing love, Dusty simply wasn't sure Blaise was the right man to commit to. These thoughts had festered during the long hours she'd spent driving the combine. Her time on the header, broken up with the trips in the truck delivering the grain to the silos about thirty minutes away.

She was pleased the barley was given malt grade and not destined for a lower price if graded feed quality for stock. It was a huge job to be doing by herself, and in what was very much a man's world.

Luckily her neighbor, Aaron Jackson, hadn't crossed her path. He was still off licking his wounds after she'd sent him packing, and Blaise had punched him one. The problem was that out here, you needed to rely on your neighbors to survive, and she hoped a time wouldn't come when she might have to call on him for help.

At least Blaise was willing to give things a go, even though it usually meant jobs took much longer since he was still very much clueless.

The niggle returned to her stomach. *Would he really stick it out here on the farm with her? It was a hard life, and just because he'd been here for a year, did that mean he would manage a forever? Why did the doubt come up like this?*

Hot air blew around her, teasing the loose strands of her light brown hair from the messy bun she'd tied it into this morning before dawn, bringing her attention back to the job at hand. She needed a sample of grain to check the moisture just to be sure. It had been an unusually cool night, and the moisture was a bit iffy this morning. Based on the hot day, she figured everything would be fine. If the moisture was too high, then when delivering the grain to the silos they could refuse it. That would be a disaster. She already had enough doubt floating around in her head, so she figured it was time to test again. Besides, it meant she'd have a bit of a break from sitting at the wheel.

Dusty forced her legs to move, ignoring the mild pins and needles in her right foot, and she made her way to the back of the harvester. The north wind's breath was strong today, and rattled the cut stalks of the wheat crop she was nearly halfway through harvesting.

The temperature kept increasing, and at this rate, it was soon going to be too hot to keep reaping. With all this machinery, a spark could easily be made, and in this heat with the crop providing fuel, the chance of a spark igniting a fire was a very real one.

So far, the day hadn't been announced by the Bureau of Meteorology, or the BOM, as being a total fire ban. Because of that, she was out trying to get the last paddock harvested before Christmas. Since Christmas was in a week, time was beginning to go against her.

There was one more paddock to harvest, the one

next to this one, and at 250 acres, this was the biggest paddock and was going to take time—more than usual, since the yields were up. But with the hot weather and potential fire bans being put into place, there was a risk that the harvest wouldn't be finished before Christmas. That was one goal her father had when he was alive—to have the crops reaped by Christmas. Dusty planned on continuing with this expectation. She didn't manage it last year, but this year she was determined to.

It meant that Christmas felt like Christmas if the harvest was completed, and it meant that she would be more relaxed and could be grateful, instead of worrying about getting it finished before the crops might end up damaged.

This year she'd put in just over the usual thousand acres of barley and wheat crops, choosing yet again not to go with canola as a crop. The yellow flowers it produced were pretty swaying in the paddocks, but the smell, well, it was like dirty socks. Plus, she needed to purchase different machinery to harvest the rapeseed crops of canola, and that was definitely not in the budget. Even with Blaise's specialized help as an accountant, there had been more of a return at tax time, but like most farms, there was always a need for more money.

Dusty picked up the empty tin she kept tucked away at the back of the combine, climbed up the ladder, her legs now remembering how to move. She opened the little hatch then scooped up some grain. It was looking good with not too much other plant rubbish in with the wheat seeds. Balancing the tin full of seeds, she closed the hatch, and clambered back down to the ground.

She went over to the truck where she kept the moisture testing unit. First, she used an ancient coffee hand grinder, it was what her grandfather had used, or so the story went. She tipped in some seeds, then turned the handle until they were a fine dust. She tipped a little into the machine—the reading was perfect—and she sighed. This was one situation where it was better to be safe than sorry, especially after this morning's reading. Just because the weather was warm didn't mean that the moisture was going to be low.

Dusty put away the testing unit, took a swig of water, and returned the tin. She climbed back into the combine once more, her muscles protesting from having to go back to the sitting position at the wheel. She moved forward a little, then stopped, flicked the level so the auger moved out over the truck, using her mirrors to ensure she was, in fact, in the right position. When she was sure everything was lined up, she hit another switch. Grain flowed like water into the truck. It would be a disaster if the grain missed the truck and spilled out on to the ground. Years of doing this job meant Dusty had a strong idea and feel of how everything aligned when dealing with such large machinery.

Yesterday, she'd taken a load to the silos, and today she wanted to fill the truck, then she would fill the paddock silos before taking another load to the silos tomorrow. It was more important to harvest the crop, but she didn't have a lot of space to store the grain, so it was a constant balancing act. With the paddock silos worth tens of thousands of dollars, and while they were a necessity, they were completely out of the budget.

A dust cloud blowing up along the tree line at the far end of the paddock caught her attention. Dusty had been in such a rush to leave this morning that she hadn't time to put together a packed lunch. All she'd managed to do was fill her water bottles, with ice then water, and grab a banana. Her stomach grumbled. She hoped her mum was bringing some food. If not, then she would use the CB radio and ask her to bring out some sandwiches.

Keeping an eye on the falling grain, she put the

combine into gear and inched forward so as the grain didn't just pile up in one spot and end up slipping over the side. She wondered if she could ever teach, let alone trust Blaise to do this one day. It would help out if he could. But then again, Blaise having a separate income would also help the daily budget.

Dusty couldn't help remembering how her father was reluctant to teach and trust her. There was a lot of money wrapped up in ensuring the grain was harvested and delivered successfully to the silos. A lot could go wrong—too much—which she knew from experience.

She smiled as a ute turned into the paddock. It was her ute. Mom had remembered. She'd meant to leave a note about the food or at least call. But once on the combine, it was too easy to keep her focus here, besides it was thoughts of Blaise that had been the distraction instead of food. Her stomach grumbled again.

The ute came closer, and she was surprised to see Blaise at the wheel, and her pure-bred Kelpie dog, Ted, on the tray, his head poking out enjoying the ride. Her border collie, Molly, peered out from the other side of the tray. The poor dogs were bored with no sheep work being done right now. Come

January with the shearing, they will be working hard.

Enjoy your little holiday now, thought Dusty.

Blaise parked in front of the combine. Dusty noted it was the worst place he could've parked. She took a very long, deep breath so as not to tell him off, and to remind herself he really was clueless. And that being patient was the only way to help educate him.

With the last of the grain transferred to the truck, she returned the auger to its nestled position on the side of the combine. She made sure everything was in park, left the engine idling, and then got down to meet Blaise.

"You found me here?" She was harvesting in one of the paddocks at the back of the farm, but the easiest way to get here was along the road.

"Of course." Blaise smiled proudly as he got out of the ute. He was wearing suit pants, a white shirt with a tie, and polished black boots which already looked like they had a layer of dust over them.

"I'm getting to know my way around."

"Mom drew you a map."

"Don't you have any faith in me? I think I'm doing more than all right in this world of farming." He stepped forward and caught her in an embrace.

Dusty's pulse increased. It had been too long since they had some intimate fun. With her focus on the harvest, there had been no time for simply *them*, and definitely no time for some bedroom fun.

His lips met hers, and Dusty's thoughts melted as his heat filled her. Her desires spiked. She ran her hands down is back. Bloody hell, he felt good. For a moment, she could almost forget about the harvest, here in his arms, his mouth on hers, lips sucking on hers, and his tongue slipping into her mouth.

Dusty made an involuntary noise of delight. Pleasure clouded her mind, and she let it take her away.

"We could... you know." He pulled away and spoke softly in her ear even though they were the only people around for miles, his hot breath tickling her skin despite the hot weather.

Dusty held her breath. She wanted him. Now. Her body was already responding with the clenching of her lower abdominal muscles with a longing to satisfy the primal need within. The hum of the idling engine behind her brought her back to reality.

"Later." It was a flippant promise, later could mean any time over the next few weeks.

Blaise sighed, not even hiding his disappointment, and it irritated her.

She was working long, hard hours. "I told you this is what it's going to be like during harvest," she spoke a little too sharply.

His eyes looked sad. "I know. And I'm being very patient."

He was.

He is.

Dusty nodded her head, wrapped her arms around his neck and pulled him into a passionate kiss. The fire of desire flamed once more through her body. "I'll make it up to you."

"You bloody better."

"It will be worth the wait, you know," she added, before giving him another kiss. If she kept this up, the kissing would end up leading to exactly what she wanted yet was putting off. No, it wasn't worth the distraction. The harvest was everything. Hell, even now standing here kissing him was wasting valuable time. She needed to step back into the combine and get this paddock reaped. The hot weather forecast could well delay her, and that would be the time for some much-needed hanky-panky with Blaise.

He sighed heavily as she broke the kiss. "Lucky for you I do know."

Dusty smiled, looked into his eyes, and for a moment nearly completely forgot herself. Then a gust of wind blew around them, pushing up a dusty cloud.

"So, tell me... why are you here, dressed up with nowhere to go?" It was like Blaise couldn't get out of the habit of dressing smartly when he was working as an accountant, even though that wasn't the expectation around here.

"Had to visit a client or two, and thought well, it's close to lunchtime, it'd be nice to see my girlfriend."

Guilt caused her stomach to twist painfully. "I appreciate the visit, sorry you're disappointed."

He clenched his jaw. "I've got a few hours to spare, and when I dropped in at the house, your mom was about to bring you some food, so I thought I'd offer to help."

The guilt double-knotted within her. He was trying, and she wasn't helping him at all.

"Thank you."

"She figured you must be hungry and in need of some caffeine."

"I am." And if she had the time, then she would attend to some other needs she had as well. "Thank you." She kissed him, then suddenly pulled away. "Sorry, I must be smelly and sweaty." She had dressed in the same work clothes as yesterday, jeans and a dark green T-shirt, wanting to save on washing. It didn't matter what she looked like or even smelled like when on the combine. Now she wished she'd at least put on fresh work clothes, not that the last few hours would've kept them clean in the slightest.

"I didn't notice." He nuzzled along the side of her neck. It was becoming harder to concentrate and to keep her resolve. She wanted to give in to him, to herself. But the harvest must come first. And if there were a total fire ban tomorrow, well, then there would be plenty of time to take the due care in having some intimate time with Blaise.

Dusty gently pushed him away. "I need to get back to it. Sorry." She hated seeing the sad puppy-dog expression on his face.

"You do? I think just a few minutes..." He bit playfully into her neck.

Her knees buckled slightly, and he easily took her weight. She wriggled out of his grasp, reluctantly.

"The harvest is nearly done, and you know I want to finish by Christmas."

"I know, though I don't see how a few minutes with me will be the reason why that won't happen."

"I want longer than a few minutes," she said softly. "I'm so sorry, but I need to focus. This is my livelihood and is part of the farm's income and survival."

He nodded, but the shadow of disappointment said otherwise.

In a moment of weakness, she had an idea. *Why not?* It would make his day if she let him. Plus, it could be a sort of compromise. A chance to spend a little time together, while still harvesting.

"Want to come for a ride?"

"Ummm... you're giving me mixed messages here, you know." He brushed the tips of his fingers up her bare arms, sending a pleasant shiver through her body.

"You have a one-track mind, don't you?"

"Not quite, but you know I haven't... well, you know, for a while." He raised his eyebrow suggestively.

Dusty laughed. "And you won't. I was referring to the combine."

His eyes lit up. "Can I?"

"Sure, come on."

He grabbed her hand stopping her from turning. "On one condition."

"You're going to have to wait." She rolled her eyes.

"That you'll let me drive."

Dusty's eyes widened at the simple request.

Can I trust him? Let him be in the driver's seat?

She swallowed hard. "You're on."

"Fantastic." He started to walk toward the combine.

"Hang on, you're not driving anywhere."

Blaise spun around. "What now?"

Dusty pointed to the ute. "You better move the bloody ute out of the way."

CHAPTER 2

Blaise cursed under his breath as he rushed to the ute. He was far from being dressed to be driving in a big, dirty machine, but to hell with that. The call to get behind the wheel of this combine was loud and clear, and he was answering.

I should've known better to park the ute here like that.

He had been thinking of how surprised Dusty was going to be to see him, and well, of course, he was hoping maybe it could lead to something else. He felt like he was in his own sort of drought because of the harvest. The seeding back in June was like this, he wasn't sure why, but with the crops, Dusty was more stressed and intense.

He patted Ted on the head. "I'm taking this as a good sign, boy. Wish me luck." Ted just looked back blankly. Molly blinked with empty eyes at him as well.

Blaise moved the ute out of the path of the combine. He wasn't sure where to park it, so he put his foot on the brake and looked around while feeling a little flustered. It was hot, he was in his suit, and it was on a whim that he'd dropped into the farm in the hopes that it would lead to seeing Dusty today. They had plans for the weekend, so she wasn't entirely avoiding him, but not seeing her as much as he was used to was becoming difficult.

It had been like this during seeding time, but he guessed he got through that because it was also the end of the financial year, and he had a lot of work. Now, for him, things were slowing down in the lead up to Christmas, which meant Blaise had a little more time on his hands. Time, he wanted to spend with Dusty. And it wasn't just the sex he was missing. He missed her laugh, her special humor, and how great he felt simply being with her, especially when they were working together on the farm. Even though it always seemed he was doing something wrong when it came to farming and Dusty. But that didn't mean he wanted to leave. He was slowly getting the hang of things. There was just so much to learn, and he was also trying to establish his own accounting business.

He put his foot on the brake, pausing to try and think of the best place to park the ute which meant it wasn't going to be in the way.

Dusty pointed in front of the truck. "Park it there for now," she yelled out.

Not where I would've thought to park it.

That was the thing, he just couldn't work out what needed to be done sometimes, no matter how much he thought about it. He did notice how tired she looked. While the shadows under her eyes weren't dark, they were there, and her eyes didn't have the sparkle they normally did. He wished he could take away some of her workload. Dusty was slowly getting better at letting him do more. She was a terrible teacher, and very impatient, which didn't help. It was one of the annoying parts about her that he secretly liked. The way her temper would rumble to the surface in a bluster, not too different from the hot north wind.

Blaise gave her the thumbs up and smiled to let her know he got it. As quickly as he could, he parked the ute and got out slamming the door. Then he remembered the packaged lunch her mom, Claire, had given him. So, he opened the door to grab the insulated lunch box then hurried over to her, not wanting to delay the harvest or be accused of it.

He didn't get the need to be in so much of a rush.

Which was why he was suggesting that they could've spend a little time together today.

"Will the dogs be fine on the back?"

"Yeah, we won't be long."

Blaise wasn't sure if 'not being long' was a good or bad thing. He decided to shrug off the comment. It didn't matter.

He was about to drive heavy machinery and looked up at the combine harvester. Though, this might just be a better option. He couldn't wait to tell his city mates, so he got out his phone and took a quick photo.

"Come on, no time for that."

He took a photo of Dusty.

"Not when I look like this."

He grinned cheekily. "I need a photo of you to remember what you look like."

"It's not like you're never going to see me again." She rolled her eyes, turned, and clambered up the metal steps and inside the cab.

Blaise had to admit, he enjoyed the sight of her tight arse in the jeans. He'd asked her why she wore jeans in such hot weather. Apparently, it was for safety reasons. Right now, he was glad about that. He certainly had a great view as she slipped into the tight space of the cab.

"Coming up?" Dusty demanded. Her facial expression was stern and lacked any sort of patience.

Blaise didn't know why, but he loved her sassy attitude. He suppressed a grin as he reached out to hold on to what he thought was a bar.

"Don't touch that."

He pulled his hand away just before his fingers touched the metal. "What?"

"You'll burn yourself." She sighed with frustration. "Weren't you watching how I got up here?"

His cheeks flamed red in a deep blush. Hell, yeah, he'd been watching.

"Blaise." She said his name in such a tone it was as if she knew what he'd really been watching. Dusty leaned out of the cab a little and pointed. "Grab on to here, and these are the steps."

"Okay." He felt a little stupid. It seemed obvious now that Dusty had shown him where he needed to hold on and where to step. He climbed up carefully, coming almost face to face with Dusty in the small space of the cab. Cool, dusty air from inside the cab filtered over him. The air conditioning unit was working overtime in this heat.

"Not a lot of room in here." He wasn't sure where to go now, and not wanting to upset Dusty, he thought he'd wait to be told what to do next. After all, he didn't want Dusty to change her mind and not let him drive the combine. He'd been hoping for a chance to get behind the wheel for a while now. Blaise wanted to drive a combine harvester and brag to his mates back in Adelaide, but more importantly, he really did want to embrace the farm life. There was a lot riding on whether he could adjust to this new world or not and whether Dusty would really let him into her life as well.

He paused and looked at her. Messy hair, dirty face, clothes smeared with dust and oil, all the result of having to work long, hard, physical hours. She was tired. Frustrated. The attraction was still there, he thought she was beautiful. A twist in his belly made him wonder if she really could go the next step of commitment with him.

With Christmas fast approaching, and the business of harvest stopping any sort of must-have conversations they needed, the doubt was increasing within him.

Dusty smiled. "I don't bite."

"You so do." He grinned, looking straight in her blue eyes. A flash of desire reflected to him, but it was gone before he was sure he'd even seen it.

"I don't mean to." She rolled her lips together as if fighting against an inner pain. He knew things had been bad, to say the least, between her neighbor and ex, Jack, and he left wounds on her soul, and even her body. It was a reminder to stay strong for her, and to be patient. No matter how hard it was getting.

"Take a seat." Dusty gestured to the dirty seat in front of the large window.

Blaise took a deep breath. The conversations they needed to have weren't the ones to have here in the combine. He grinned and shimmied past her, making sure his body brushed against hers as much as possible. Shivers of pleasure coursed through him with a longing that was hard to ignore.

Dusty took the bag of food from him.

He plonked himself in the seat, and it bounced up and down.

"Wow! Great suspension." Blaise naturally put his hands on the steering wheel. He grinned. It was a little boy's dream coming true.

"Well, it is needed. The paddock isn't smooth like the roads you're used to." Dusty reached out of the cab, grabbed the handle of the door, and with her body weight behind her pulled it shut with a force that caused Blaise to jump.

Dusty shuffled over to behind the side of the seat. There was no room for two people here, so it forced them together.

"How do I accelerate?" Blaise couldn't wait to get driving. A quick glance at the controls made it clear he had absolutely no idea of how to drive the combine.

Dusty leaned over him and flicked some switches. The combine jerked as if in gear.

"Gently push on that lever there."

Blaise braced himself, held his breath, and did exactly as he was instructed. The combine rolled forward. His body prickled with excitement, and he suppressed a whooping that he wanted to yell out. He was driving big machinery, so he needed to concentrate.

"Where do I go?" Blaise looked around, glad they were in a paddock with plenty of room. He wasn't sure how Dusty managed to park the combine in the shed.

A flutter of nerves moved in his belly. *I got this.*

"See over there, the crop is a bit higher."

"Oh yeah." It seemed obvious now that she'd

pointed it out. He steered the combine over to the crop.

"Do I just start anywhere? Shouldn't I go from where you left off." He'd learned a little from when driving the tractor during seeding, but this was so different.

"No, just start here, it will work out in the end. The point is to reap the crop, not have straight rows like when seeding." He cringed. When driving the tractor with the seeder hooked up at the back, his rows hadn't been very straight. Dusty had promptly sent him back to the house. This time he wanted to prove to her he could do this. He could be hands-on with farm life. His motivation went deeper, he also wanted to prove it to himself.

"I can drive to the where you stopped," he suggested. He was finding it hard to concentrate. Driving was taking all of his brainpower.

How does she do this?

"You'll waste diesel getting to that point," said Dusty.

There it was again, another reference to ensure money isn't wasted. It always amused Blaise how tight everything was on the farm with money. He was an accountant and tight himself, but life on the farm took things to an entirely new level. Blaise understood, especially when he offered to secretly do the farm's accounts with Dusty's mom nearly two years ago. He had saved them a lot on returns, which gave them a bit of breathing space financially. A good crop this year would help them maybe get a little in front.

Could I live like this year to year?

"Just keep going straight, then turn right, easing the header, the part where the blades are moving to cut the stalks into the crop." Dusty instructions interrupted his thoughts. "And you can go a bit faster, you know."

"I think I'm going fast enough." Suddenly, he realized he was driving the combine, by himself, and Dusty hadn't actually given him a lesson. I needed a lesson. His stomach knotted with threads of panic. This was another part of farm life he was having to adjust to big time. Sure, he got lessons, and explanations, but sometimes he was thrown into the deep end and expected to swim, old-school style.

"Will the header thing just start working." Blaise could feel himself beginning to become stressed. "How do I do that?"

Dusty chuckled softly. "I'll help you. It takes too much to explain, and you won't learn it all on your first go."

"Okay, and that's meant to make me feel better right now?"

"You're doing fine."

Her words helped to ease the tension within him and boost his confidence. That was big praise coming from Dusty.

The crop was close now, he could see the individual stalks. "Should I start to turn now?"

"Yes, see you're a natural."

Blaise turned the wheel to the right slowly. The header was getting close to the crop. Panic began to rise inside of him. He felt like there was something he needed to do, but of course, he didn't know and had to rely on Dusty. "What should I do?"

"Don't panic." Dusty reached over behind him. "Concentrate. I'll lower the header down this time for you. Just line up the crop and slowly go deeper until the header is full."

It sounded way too easy to be true for Blaise. He held his breath, doing exactly what Dusty had told him. She moved a lever. The header lowered closer to the ground and began to rotate.

Shit, this is real.

He was about to harvest for the first time.

Sweat beaded on his forehead, despite the coolness of the air conditioner.

"Move a bit further into the crop."

He adjusted. Looking down in front, seeing the stalks begin to fill the header, the blades moving quickly which made him nervous. At thirty feet long it took a few seconds for him to line up the combine, so the header was full of the stalks. The rotating blade made quick work of the long stalks, chopping them off, and pushing them back into the machinery where they would be thrashed and the valuable seeds collected.

"Steady."

Blaise kept his focus, staring firmly at the edge of the crop to ensure it was filling the header and not leaving any behind. There was a lot riding on him right now, and he felt every bit of that pressure.

"You're a natural."

Blaise smiled. Another big compliment from Dusty. Maybe things were slowly beginning to change with her.

"Should I ask what the pay rate is?" Blaise dared to take his eyes off the front of the combine for a moment.

Dusty sighed. Reached over and turned the steering wheel.

What? Blaise sat stunned for a moment.

"Look out the rearview mirror. There." Dusty pointed to the mirror on the left.

Blaise glanced out.

"See the bit of crop you left behind."

Blaise saw it. "Yes."

"That's your pay."

A sinking feeling hit Blaise's stomach. Damn! It hadn't taken him long before he messed up.

"Sorry."

"You're learning." The words she spoke were tight and edgy as if she was holding back her temper.

Blaise gripped the steering wheel tightly, his knuckles whitening. "Do you want me to stop?"

"You can finish going around once."

"Really?" Blaise had been bracing for her to make him stop and to kick him out. He'd missed a chunk of crop. "I can go back for the bit I missed."

"Wastes too much diesel, it's not worth it."

"Okay." He knew the cost analysis very well as an accountant, but this was a whole new level.

"Keep focussed, you're learning."

Blaise nodded his head. He kept his concentration on the edge of the crop, determined to get it right. He didn't even think of Dusty standing behind him.

"Okay, slow down, you've done one lap."

Blaise exhaled, and slowed the combine. He hadn't even noticed he'd finished a lap—that's how much he was in deep concentration.

Dusty helped guide him to stop the combine.

"Do I get the sack?"

"Hmmm... just not paid."

With that, Blaise decided there was progress. "Thanks for letting me drive."

Dusty smiled and opened the door of the cab. "You okay to get to the ute? You remember, only drive on the fire breaks when you leave."

"I will." Blaise stood, his legs felt like jelly, and his body ached after the short time in the cramped position at the wheel. He shimmied in front of Dusty, paused, looking into her eyes. *Had this been a good or bad thing?* He wasn't sure.

Dusty gave him a quick kiss on the cheek. "I'll see you later."

Blaise got the hint. He kissed her back, quickly, on the cheek, and then carefully climbed down. He looked up, Dusty waved, then closed the door.

He walked to the back of the combine, and out of the way. His legs struggling to want to work properly as his muscles got used to not being in the same position.

The combine started rolling forward, the roar of the engine loud and disruptive in this natural setting of wide-open spaces.

Blaise made his way through the stubble, to the ute, and got in. Dusty hadn't gotten angry with him like she often did, and it unsettled Blaise. It gave him hope that they could both adjust to each other. But then again, was it a sign that maybe she'd given up?

He wasn't ready to give up on them. He may well have messed up in Dusty's eyes just then, but by driving the combine for a short time, he now had a renewed admiration for the work she had to do on the farm. He took a deep breath. The short time driving had left him exhausted. He put the ute into gear and slowly made his way out of the paddock, carefully keeping to the fire break. The last thing he wanted to do was to cause a spark which resulted in a bush fire. It had been drilled into him over the last few months, in particular.

No wonder Dusty looked exhausted. Yet, she kept on going.

This insight gave him much-needed motivation to keep on this path, to keep chasing his dusty cloud in the name of love.

CHAPTER 3

Blaise drove back along the unsealed road toward Acacia Plains. Dust blew up behind him in a smoky-like cloud. He'd never realized how much it didn't rain now he was here living in the country. In the city, the rain tended to be more of a nuisance more than anything. Of course, out here on the land, it could make or break people.

It was later in the day than expected, and he had planned on going back to the place he'd rented. Dusty had said she'd see him later. What annoyed him about the ambiguity was that it could translate to later being tonight, or tomorrow, or hell even Christmas at this rate. He'd never thought to ask her to commit to a time.

The quick drive in the combine at least gave him

the empathy he needed to be unforgiving about her lack of commitment. He'd been open-minded coming here to the country to live, to trial having a relationship with Dusty. What he hadn't quite been prepared for was that he was also having to develop a relationship to the farm as well.

Blaise looked ahead at the straight road. Eucalyptus trees lined either side, along with low-lying bushes he had no idea what their names were. He had a vague recollection Dusty had called them tea trees, *Leptospermum*. When they were moving a mob to a different paddock the other month, he'd sat in the passenger seat, and she'd named the species of trees and plants as if she were a botanist, and he'd been impressed. Long weedy dried grasses swayed as he passed. Even at his reduced speed, he couldn't bring himself to drive fast on these dirt roads, not like the locals did.

A magpie flew across the road, followed by a few swallows which were considered pests. Blaise couldn't believe how much he had learned, and how much he noticed around him even when he was driving. He enjoyed the change, and it gave him hope, reminding him he was adjusting. So often it felt like he wasn't and that he knew nothing.

A banging noise started at the back of the ute.

Blaise fought against the steering wheel to stop the car from veering toward the bank of the road. He automatically took his foot off the accelerator, and hearing Dusty's voice resisted the urge to brake. There were sections of loose stone on this road and braking could send him into a skid into the nearest tree.

Blaise held his breath as the ute skidded a little, then slowed, the thumping got worse, before the ute finally stopped. He exhaled with relief. This was one time Blaise was glad he didn't drive fast on these roads. Dusty did, which was fine, she'd grown up and could read them, and knew the conditions and how to adjust. All he saw was dirt and potholes.

He got out of the ute, barely noticing the heat of the afternoon.

What the hell was that?

His legs were a little like jelly as he walked around the back of the ute trying to see anything obvious that might've caused the noise and affected the steering. For a gut-wrenching moment, he thought something very bad might've happened to Ted or Molly. The dogs were sitting on the tray of the ute, chained safety, and looking rather bored.

"Glad you're all right, boy." Blaise patted Ted, happy the dog was fine. Molly barked at him as if telling him off for ignoring her. He smiled. "And you too, girl."

He didn't want to be the one to tell Dusty he'd killed Ted or Molly. That would surely end any chance of a future relationship with each other.

Knowing that Ted and Molly were fine, he focussed his attention on the ute. He'd been worried about damaging the ute knowing how tight money was for Dusty and her mom, and an accident in the ute would stress them financially.

The tailgate of the tray was secure which he thought might've been the cause. With no idea what he was looking for, he kept moving until he came to the front passenger side.

For Fuck's sake. He sighed heavily. It was a flat tire. *Of course.*

This was when he wished he could call the local roadside service, the RAA. They did come out here, but he knew damn well he'd be laughed at if he called them for a flat tire. There was no way he was going to ask Dusty for help, she needed to finish reaping that paddock. He wasn't about to be the one to delay her. Her mom, Claire, might be the person to ask, but then again, she was going into Wilkton this afternoon, so she wasn't at the farmhouse right now.

Looks like it's me and the ute.

He looked at the very flat tire.

Sure, he knew how to change them, he just wasn't sure how to on this vehicle.

Welcome to country life, hey, he thought to himself as he searched through the ute looking for a jack. *Learn as you go and hope for the best.* That was exactly what he was doing now and rescheduling the afternoon's plans. He wasn't going to get the accounts done for the Bakers and Hancocks, after all. Let alone get to Bluey's Mechanics long, overdue accounts. He wasn't sure why, but he seemed to attract clients whose accounting was behind or in an utter mess.

The spare tire was under the tray, and he wasn't sure how he was going to get that out.

He looked down at his suit.

Yeah, I gotta get better clothing.

Though he wasn't sure what his clients would think now if he turned up in jeans and a shirt, or even if he wore some Wrangler or Rossi clothing the country folk dressed in. He'd been persisting in dressing in his city-style suits all year. It was the clothing he owned, and he wanted to look professional and make an impression. Not for the first time, he wondered what sort of impression he was really making.

Blaise managed to find the jack behind the passenger seat. *There you are.* One step done. He put it on the ground. Now, how the hell was he going to get the tire out?

"You any good at changing tires?" he asked the dogs. They'd both laid down in the back of the ute and had settled for a long nap. "Yeah, didn't think so."

At the back of the ute, Blaise squatted to try and work out how to get the tire out. Everything was thick with dust. He attempted to unscrew some bolts but they were seized with the dust.

Fuck it.

He got some tools out of the ute, and tried again, but nothing was budging.

Fuck.

This wasn't going to be easy. In fact, he was beginning to think it could well be impossible for him. While it was just a tire, it was also a chance to prove he could problem solve in a situation like this.

Blaise gave the bolts another turn, but hey still didn't move. He put all his weight behind the movement, pushing hard, his feet moving in the dirt instead. In frustration, he stood and kicked the tire.

The dogs looked up at him as if annoyed he'd disturbed their sleep.

The rumble of an approaching vehicle made Blaise look up and behind him. He could do with some help. Even though it would be good to tell Dusty he changed the tire by himself, he wasn't about to knock back another pair of hands.

Blaise saw a ute come into focus further along the road behind him. As it approached his heart sank. He knew who owned that ute, and he didn't want it to stop.

Fucking Aaron.

The ute stopped next to Blaise's, blocking the road. Aaron wound down the passenger door window, leaned over and yelled out to Blaise, "In a bit of bother?"

"Nothing I can't handle," Blaise called back.

He would never trust Aaron, especially not after he had hit Dusty. They'd come to blows themselves, and it had cost Blaise his job in Adelaide. But, at least, that had a silver lining to it as he was now here in Wilkton, and he was in a relationship with Dusty. Aaron was the annoying ex, who was a neighbor, and Blaise was still coming to terms with having to see him around town. He didn't think he would ever get used to it.

"Really? I must say I'm surprised you're still here."

The grin on Aaron's face caused Blaise to cringe, but he squared his shoulders and glared back. "It's only a flat tire. I'll have it changed in no time."

Aaron chuckled dryly. "I would've thought the likes of you would've gone back to Adelaide by now."

"And why is that?" A chill went through Blaise, he didn't like where this conversation was heading. While he was still getting used to the country banter, this was something more coming from Aaron.

"Ahhh, well, you know... city boy like you living out here is one thing. But dating a someone like Dusty, I'm surprised she hasn't kicked your ass out."

Blaise darkened his glare at Aaron.

"Oh, right, I forgot. You're not living together, are you?"

Asshole. Blaise clenched his jaw tightly to stop himself from responding. He knew Aaron was baiting him, and it took all his self-control not to bite back.

"Here, I'll show you there's no ill-feeling. After all, what are neighbors for? Gotta put our differences aside and help each other."

Much to Blaise's annoyance, Aaron turned the engine off and got out. Blaise knew he needed help, but he sure as hell didn't want that help to come from Aaron. He didn't care if he were there all afternoon trying to change this bloody tire. Besides, surely someone else might come along and give him a hand. The chances of that happened had to be in his favor.

Aaron kneeled at the back of the ute. "These old utes are tricky. You got to loosen it here first."

Blaise clenched his jaw. He hated how easily Aaron got the tire out. He was on edge after the comments about him and Dusty. *He had some nerve talking like that.*

"Where's the jack? Oh, I see it."

In no time at all, Aaron had the ute jacked up and was undoing the nuts on the wheel. Blaise struggled to find the words to tell Aaron to get on his way and not to punch him one. Hell, Aaron deserved a punch or two just for being Aaron. Blaise flexed his right hand as he stood next to him, feeling a bit like a third wheel. Not for one moment did Blaise think that Aaron was doing this out of the kindness of his heart. Then he realized what Aaron was really up to.

Bastard.

For the next few weeks he wouldn't be going to the local pub, Ol' Billies, because of the ribbing he'd get from the other men about not being able to change a tire.

Looks like frozen meals for me for a while.

That or maybe he would stay at the farm. He shifted uneasily on his feet at the thought. Aaron's words had hit a raw nerve. Even though Blaise had been here for nearly a year, and while the relationship had its bumps, everything was going well enough with Dusty. The thing that was beginning to get to him was that he'd never spent more than one night in a row at her farm. Even then, he'd only stayed over a few times. Dusty always blamed her mom being there, so when he did happen to stay over, it was when she'd gone to Adelaide to visit Dusty's sister, Jody.

It was becoming crunch time.

The time when he moved in with her or moved on.

He didn't want the latter.

With the business of harvest, he wasn't able to have the conversation with Dusty to sort the issues out. He was beginning to worry if she'd ever have the time. There was Christmas and New Year, and he really didn't want to have such a conversation then because what if it ended badly? Then future Christmases and New Years would be ruined by the bad memory. If he waited until January, then it would be shearing. There was always going to be something which got in the way.

He looked down at Aaron as he took off the flat tire and realized even Aaron was getting in the way of him and Dusty.

"Here, let me help you, it's heavy," said Blaise, his words aimed to have a dig at Aaron. He'd kept up his gym visits, it helped to blow off a lot of steam from sitting all day at the computer balancing figures.

"Nah, I got it." Aaron moved in front of Blaise to stop him from helping. "Don't want to break a nail."

I'd happily break every one of them, if it's from punching you. Blaise inhaled to stop his temper from erupting.

Aaron hauled the tire on to the back of the ute, just missing Molly.

Ted growled at Aaron.

"Good boy, Ted." Blaise couldn't help praising Ted, who at this point was showing he had an excellent judge of character.

"Never liked that dog," grumbled Aaron.

"Can't see why," said Blaise sarcastically. This day wasn't going at all well. He wanted to get back to his place. *Maybe if I hung around at the farm I might get to see Dusty.* The thought was encouraging. *She might be vague about when we will see each other next, but I can make sure it's sooner rather than later.*

Aaron replaced the tire and started refixing the bolts. "You know Dusty will never let you move into the farm with her."

Not this again. Another chill went through Blaise. He hated these sorts of games.

"It's none of your business," Blaise said bluntly.

"She needs someone who knows what they're doing." Aaron fixed the last bolt tightly.

I know what I'm doing—

Aaron interrupted his thought by saying, "On the farm." Aaron looked snidely down his nose at Blaise.

'Course that's what you meant.

"She needs someone who can actually help her and not just bring her lunches."

"You spying on us?" Blaise narrowed his eyes at Aaron.

He chuckled. "Oh, so, I'm right. Well, there you go. You're doing the women's work and bringing the lunches. How damn quaint. It's good Claire has a bit of a break."

"You should get on your way." Blaise wasn't sure if he were going to be able to hold back from punching Aaron if this bullshit kept up.

"I guess my work here is done." Aaron raise an

eyebrow. "It won't work out, you two aren't from the same worlds, and despite what you might think, I can wait patiently. She'll come around and back to me. You wait and see."

"Like hell she will." Blaise could feel the heat in his blood begin to reach boiling point. Aaron may well have helped changed the tire, but he had ulterior motives which were setting him on edge.

"You never know, and based on your reaction, I'm on the money." He stood. "No worries about fixing your tire, you can buy me a beer at the pub when you're in next."

"Sure," Blaise lied. There was no way he was about to buy Aaron a beer, not after what he's insinuating. "We can reminisce on old times."

"Say hi to Dusty for me." Aaron got into his ute, started the engine, and pumped the accelerator a few times for good measure.

Blaise stood, angry, blood boiling as he watched Aaron drive away. *Wanker.*

The problem was, all that Aaron had said had rung true about how Blaise was really feeling about his relationship with Dusty. He tried to remind himself as the dust settled on the road, when driving the combine she hadn't got angry with him when he messed up. At least, not as dramatically as she had in the past. But it just felt like there was something between them which wasn't going to let them have a future together.

Would Dusty commit to the next step in their relationship?

Would she let him move in with her?

The potential answers scared the hell out of Blaise.

CHAPTER 4

The sun was sinking fast, approaching the horizon much quicker than Dusty would've liked. She suppressed a yawn and refocussed. She was so close to completing this paddock.

To keep herself amused working such long hours, she was having a competition with the sun. At least it was a focus.

The packed lunch had been eaten hours ago and also the extra snacks her mom had included. Dusty had tried to make the silverside and corn relish sandwiches last longer into the afternoon, but a combination of hunger, exhaustion, and boredom meant that she'd given in to the temptation to eat them. The pumpkin scones were delish, freshly baked this morning by her mom, though she wished they had a little bit of butter on them and were warm. That's how she really liked to eat pumpkin scones. The handful of hard-boiled lollies were a little pick-me-up. Dusty almost felt like she was back at school eating a packed lunch and finding the sweets her mom had given as a treat.

She'd drunk all the black tea her mom had provided which was full of sugar. It was a tradition started by her dad, Sam, as that was how he liked his tea. It had arrived hot, but she left it too cool, just the way to drink it on a hot day. About an hour ago she'd finished the last of the water in her water bottle.

Dinner had passed, and she knew her mom would bring out more food, but only if she asked her to. Dusty didn't want to bother her. Or Blaise. Heck, he would drive back from Wilkton to help if she asked. She assumed he would be back in town by now.

That was the thing.

She didn't want to ask.

He was trying to set up his accounting business, and she wanted it to be a success for him. He'd given up enough to come here for them. Anyway, she needed to stand on her own two feet with the running of the farm, something she could do very well, even though it was tough at times.

Dusty made another turn around the paddock. She could see the other side of the crop, swaying in the breeze which was now picking up. Thank goodness the heat hadn't peaked as high as predicted by the Bureau of Meteorology. She really wanted to get this paddock reaped and to move on to the last paddock, by the other side of the house. It was much easier working closer to the farmhouse, instead of miles away.

Their property was spread out in three sections, and the land didn't join which made more work transporting heavy machinery along the dirt roads as well as moving flock of sheep during the year.

Three more rounds will do it.

The rounds were short, but it was beginning to drive her a bit batty having to go in circles like she did in the combine. This always happened late in the season when nearing the end, and she was worn out from the long hours of sitting on the tractor. It was more than simply sitting, there was a lot to concentrate on when driving something as huge as the combine harvester.

Dusty wondered if Blaise understood that. At least he wasn't being over-demanding for her attention at the moment. She couldn't deal with that. While she did miss him and wanted to spend more time with him, but the farm came first.

Would that be a deal-breaker for him?

She found it hard to imagine a future with him. Her gut churned. She did want a future with him, but her mind couldn't get over the differences between them and the practical side of it. *Would he really be satisfied in the long term living isolated on a farm when he was used to life in the city and hearing his neighbors coughing next door?* That was the answer she really wasn't sure of. So many times during the last year, he'd stepped up and helped and kept giving things a go. The fact he didn't give up made her want him even more. He was willing to stand next to her, so much more than Aaron was ever able to do. All he ever wanted was to dominate her. No, there was no reason to think of Aaron anymore. Blaise was so much more of a man than he is, even if he had no idea how to farm and stood out like dog's balls here in the country.

Was this the answer she needed so she and Blaise could go forward? Knowing that he was a better man than Aaron.

Dusty glanced outside checking the fading light at the header and moving blades.

Fuck.

She swerved the wheel to make sure she didn't miss the crop. When her concentration broke like this, she knew it was time for a break.

Or more.

Time to stop.

Dusty wasn't about to stop.

She kept harvesting on account of being so close to finishing.

Half an hour at most, and this paddock would be reaped. More so then, she could drive the combine back to the farmyard, ready to refuel in the morning before going on to the last paddock.

With a sigh of relief, Dusty completed the last round, which was more like a strip now, saving herself an extra turn around. Pleased she'd judged it well in the fading light and while being tired, she drove back to the truck to empty the combine bin.

Feeling satisfied with her efforts and with the last paddock a sure thing to be reaped before Christmas, Dusty drove the combine back to Acacia Plains.

BLAISE SHUT the chook shed door with a firm bang, ensuring it was secure. The chooks quietly clucking to themselves as the lucky ones sat in the nesting boxes, and the others perched with the rooster on the thick, rusted horizontal piping Dusty's dad had erected. He enjoyed hearing the stories about the history of the farm. Since it had only been a few years since Dusty's dad had passed, he thought it brave she could be so open to him.

At least she's open with me sometimes. The thought squeezed his heart.

The afternoon had been a long one for Blaise after the incident with Aaron. It was as if all the doubt he'd had about the relationship with Dusty was brought to mind, and he couldn't shake it.

He'd driven the ute back to the farm and met Claire, who was about to go into town. Blaise thought it a little odd she wasn't saying what for as she normally did. Sometimes it was grocery shopping, others for the craft group, then there was the coffee catch-up with friends, even doctor appointments. This time, she was keeping silent about what this trip was really about.

Blaise told her about the flat tire in the ute. He didn't mention Aaron, though the thought of that man kept his blood running hot with anger.

Deciding to take the tire in now, he transferred it to the back of her Holden car, and Claire would take it in to be fixed. It meant one less job for Dusty to do. If she wasn't about to let him help with the big jobs, then he would do the little ones. At least, he hoped it would help.

Claire invited him to stay for the afternoon. After the incident with Aaron, Blaise agreed. He figured it was better to hang around, instead of driving back to his place in Wilkton. By being at the farm he was more likely to catch up with Dusty later. This afternoon's brief encounter had left him wanting to simply spend time with her, reconnect, laugh, and enjoy each other's company.

He'd set up his computer on the kitchen table, managing to work on some of his accountancy projects. The figures at least offered a distraction to the thoughts about him and Dusty and where they were heading. *Together? Apart?* He couldn't tell what was in front and it was making him nervous.

Before he knew it, the sun was setting, and Claire was back from Wilkton telling him to stay for dinner. *What could he do?* There was no way he was about to decline a home-cooked meal from Claire, especially since she was going to put together a roast meal. He did wish that he had some clean clothes to change into. If he could leave some clothes here, that would help. So far, Dusty hadn't made him feel welcome enough to do that. Besides, with Claire here all the time, Dusty was reluctant to let anything happen, and he spent more time in town at his place. He got it. He would feel the same. But still, it felt like they were at the crossroads in their relationship with both of them needing to make the decision of which direction to take.

To make himself useful, he insisted he did the evening jobs. With Ted and Molly's help, he'd penned the show team, the merino ewes and rams that Dusty would give extra care for sale in the on-property auction next year and for exhibiting in the country shows. The community's focus around the country shows was another new experience for him. He had no idea that it was a thing with Dusty busy entering the sheep and Claire cooking up a storm with her entries for the Wilkton show had been a lot of fun in August.

Am I really settling into this life? He hated how Aaron too easily made him feel uneasy about this.

I am, he told himself firmly.

Bucket in hand full of a dozen brown eggs laid during the day, he walked back to the house using the light of his phone to help guide him.

The pine trees swayed in the evening breeze, the heat of the day still lingering heavily in the air. The smell of the animals was not something he detested after being around them anymore. When he'd first moved here, he'd found the odors difficult to ignore. He smiled to himself. It was all now quite normal to him.

What a change for a city boy, he thought to himself.

Here he was doing the daily chores as if he'd been doing them all his life.

Blaise walked past Ted and Molly's pens. They were happily chewing on a bone he'd given them. He grinned thinking that all they needed for Christmas was a bone, and they'd be happy.

That reminded him, he had no idea what he was going to get Dusty. That decision paled in comparison to the one needing to be made, at what exactly the Christmas plans were going to be for the two of them. His parents were wanting to see him, which of course was fine, but what he wanted was to spend Christmas with Dusty.

The question was, where was Christmas going to be this year?

Here at Acacia Plains or back in Adelaide?

On the day, or will it need to be delayed?

Blaise hated not being able to make these decisions, and to be left in limbo for what was going to be their first Christmas together concerned him. He was worried that the harvest might just make this not the special time together of bonding that he was yearning for.

He approached the backyard. Light streaming from the back door helped to guide him in the dark.

A rumbling engine and bright light caught his attention. He turned to his left and saw the combine bumping slowly past the shearing shed.

Blaise grinned to himself, his pulse increased. The combine here in the yard hopefully meant that Dusty was finished for the night, and that by hanging around, he was going to be rewarded by spending some time with her. He left the bucket of eggs by the back gate, hanging on a post, and walked toward the combine. He had to know if she'd finished for the day or not. For selfish reasons, he hoped she had.

Keeping close to the shed in case Dusty didn't see him in the darkness, Blaise waited for the combine to stop. He was clutching to the slither of hope that they could share a meal together tonight, even if Claire was there. He didn't mind Dusty's mom, in fact, he found her a lot of fun.

Bang!

The combine jerked and came to a stop near the fuel tanks.

Blaise jumped. *What the fuck was that?*

He rushed over to the combine hoping Dusty was all right. His mind raced. The engine was still running. There was no smell of fire, which he took as a good thing. There was a bit of a greasy metal smell, but he wasn't sure if that was normal or not.

The door of the cab swung open. Dusty clambered down, her feet barely touching the ground.

"Are you okay?" he asked.

"Yeah." She rushed around to the back.

"You sure?" Blaise followed her.

"Fuck. Not now," cursed Dusty.

"What?"

"Bloody bearing broke."

He pressed his lips together to stop himself from asking what a bearing was. Based on Dusty's reaction, it meant it was obviously a very bad thing to break.

"I'm sure Bluey will come out in the morning and fix it." Dusty sighed heavily.

Blaise wanted to go up to her and put his hand around her waist to pull her into an embrace. He didn't dare. He wasn't sure if right now she was about to explode or not. Instead, he tried to think of something to say that would calm her down.

"You'll be out in the paddock in no time, I'm sure."

Dusty ran her hand through her hair. "This is bad."

"How bad?"

"Bad. I don't know if I'll finish before Christmas now."

Blaise thought she was jumping to the wrong conclusion, but he kept quiet. "Can you ring Bluey now?"

"I want to." She inhaled slowly, looking at the combine.

Blaise wasn't exactly sure what at. "But...?"

"Too late tonight."

"In the morning then."

She let out a frustrated sigh. "A breakdown like this is going to be a big cost, not just money, but time, too. I can't afford either right now."

"Dusty, I'm sure he'll fix it, and you'll be back on the combine before you know it."

"Sometimes machinery isn't so easily fixed." She put her hands on her hips.

"How about you finish up here, come inside, and we can talk about it over dinner."

She glared at him, and Blaise immediately knew he'd said the wrong thing.

"Don't you want to spend time with me?" The words were said before he could filter them in his mind.

"No... I mean, yes."

Blaise felt his chest tighten. "What way is it, Dusty?" He was fast losing his patience.

"You're right. Dinner with you tonight will be good. I need a break."

His breathing eased.

"I need to do the jobs first."

"Done." Blaise squared his shoulders proudly.

"Really?"

"Yeah. I was heading back from shutting up the chooks when I saw you coming into the yard."

"Thank you."

"You can thank me later." He winked.

"Or now."

Before he could answer, her lips were on his, hot and salty, her tongue dancing over his, her hands around his neck. She was finally in his arms, and he didn't want to let go.

DUSTY FELT the tension in her body begin to ease as her lips moved with his. Blaise wrapped his arms around her waist and pulled her into him. It was as if his strength enveloped her, and his heat melted away the worry of harvest. She could feel his hardness pressing into her. Her intimate muscles clenched with desire.

Why have I been so stupid to deny him? He was here. Supporting her. Wanting her.

It was a lot more than any countryman she'd previously dated.

The walls around her heart melted a little more as she pushed her hands up under his shirt, feeling his strong back. He moaned with desire. Their kiss deepened. She could feel her moisture thickening, dampening her panties, the desire to be with him flaming hot with need.

The engine of the combine hummed loudly behind them.

"Should you turn it off?" he asked.

"Needs to cool down for a few minutes."

"Then we have some time?"

"We have more than some time." Dusty let herself give in to her desires. Her mind dizzied pleasantly.

"Here?"

She took his hand and walked him over to the shed. She opened the ute, grabbed the picnic blanket she kept behind the seat, and spread it out over the hay in the corner.

She turned to him. "Where were we?"

His hands traced up her bare arms, sending her wild with sparks of desire. "About here." He ran his hand along her jawline, down her neck, his lips finding hers once more. His hands continued down her chest, over her breast, leaving a trail of heat that woke her body sexually, and she shivered heavily.

"Too much for you?" he asked cheekily.

"Fuck, no. Keep going or I'll have to kick your butt."

"I have no intention of stopping," he whispered, his breath hot in her ear. "Or getting my butt kicked."

He cupped his hand over her breast and squeezed until she gasped with the perfect mix of delight and discomfort. She pushed her body into his, wanting to feel all of him. She tugged at the buttons of his shirt, expertly undoing them, then pushing the material off his shoulders, letting it fall away.

She let her hands roam over his taut chest muscles enjoying his smooth skin. The tips of her fingers finding the soft hair which led down under his jeans.

He brushed her fingers away. "I'm enjoying you first," he mumbled as he pushed up her T-shirt, exposing her stomach. He kissed her skin, his mouth moist and hot on her soft belly. She moaned with encouragement, wanting more, but trying to hold back to enjoy the journey of reaching her peak.

She grabbed the bottom of her T-shirt and pulled it over her head, dropping it casually as her hands longed to keep touching his body.

His hands traced the bottom of her lacy bra, slipping over her breasts before stretching the material to expose her hardening nipples. She arched her chest out, giving him full access to pleasure her. His mouth cupped a nipple, tongue flicking hard against it. A bolt of desire sent a wave of fresh moisture pooling in her panties. She lifted her leg, wrapping it around his waist, bringing his hard groin closer to her. Her hips ground into his.

"I want you in me." She breathed heavily, fighting against the fast-approaching peak she was moving toward.

"In good time." He unbuttoned her jeans, then pushed the denim over her hips. She kicked off her boots and slipped out of her jeans.

He pulled her into him, her breasts crushing pleasantly against his bare chest. His hands moved over her buttocks, gripping and pulling them up, tightening her pussy with the motion.

He slipped his hand over the front of her hip, brushing against the lace of her panties, over her mound, before pushing the material away to dip his fingers into her fleshy folds.

Her body jerked from the pleasure of his touch between her legs and the stroking motion of her pussy, as he built the tension within her. She could feel a mini orgasm taking hold, and her body convulsed as it burst, sending pleasure pulsating through her. Her breath quickened from the bliss flooding through her.

He pushed down her panties, his mouth pressed into her mound, tongue flicked along her length, sending her mind back into the dizzying heights of ecstasy. She put her hands on his head to keep her balance as he worked her back toward losing control. With a long gasp, she felt the orgasm take over fully this time, opening a flood of desire.

He moved away, stood, and helped her to the ground.

She breathed heavily. The moisture thick

between her legs from the pleasure he'd teased from her body.

He stood and took off his jeans and jocks. She looked up seeing his cock, hard and pulsing as he kneeled over, positioning himself at her entrance. She could feel his hot tip pushing into her opening while her hips arched, wanting him to fill her. He pushed in, her muscles contracting wildly around his cock. He groaned, paused for a moment, then slowly slid back out before entering her again.

Noises of pleasure came from her as he moved himself in and out. This time the orgasm ripped through them both as they clutched onto each other.

He eased himself from her and settled next to her. She wrapped her arms around him, enjoying feeling his naked body next to hers in the afterglow they'd created.

"Tonight was just a taste, you know?" Dusty kissed him softly on the lips.

"Well, I enjoyed my entrée, and I'm looking forward to when I might get my main course and dessert."

"Oh, expecting a three-course meal?"

Blaise chuckled. "Absolutely." He nuzzled along the side of her neck, enjoying the shiver it caused in her.

"You're too good for me," she mumbled in an absentminded tone.

"Likewise, you know."

"Hmmm... what a pair we are."

He kissed her. "Does that mean I can move in?"

"I don't know." Her stomach churned.

"Dusty..." His voice soft, full of disappointment.

She wasn't at all good at having conversations after they'd had sex. It was as if her mind was all muddled from the bliss or something.

"Just... I .... we need to talk about what this means. And you know—"

"Dusty? You out there? Dinner's getting cold."

"Fuck." Dusty jumped up and started to grab her clothes. "We can't let Mom find us like this."

"We took a little too long?" Blaise bolted upright.

"A little."

He reached up and grabbed her arm, pulling her back down. "We need to have this conversation, you know?"

The flutter of fear she felt few away when she looked into his eyes. "I know."

"Blaise, you out there, too?" called Clare loudly.

"Shit," said Blaise.

"Come on, I'll turn off the engine of the combine, and then we better go in for dinner before Mom comes looking for us." Dusty shimmied on her dirty jeans glancing at Blaise while he dressed. He grinned at her, and warmth built inside of her.

It had been difficult to let the last of the walls down around her heart, but she was so glad she did.

Could she take the next step with him?

She hated how the question lingered, and the answer always felt so far out of her reach.

CHAPTER 5

"Another delicious meal, thank you." Blaise put his spoon onto the plate, a floral design around the edge. It amused him that Claire brought out the best china whenever he ate with them. The apple pie and fresh cream had been nothing like he'd eaten before. He was glad he'd taken out a gym membership here at Wilkton, otherwise with all this great home-cooked food, he'd be packing on the pounds.

"I'll help you clean the dishes." Blaise stood from the chair at the kitchen table where he, Dusty, and her mom had been eating their very late dinner.

"You will not." Claire waved her finger at him. "You two should go into the living room. I'll clean up."

"Mom, I can help. It won't take long."

Claire opened her mouth as if to say no.

Blaise interjected. "Good idea. If we all help, then it will be a lot quicker. You've had a big day, too." He took his plate to the sink and began running the water to start washing the dishes.

"Did you Mom? What did you get up to?" Dusty collected her mom's plate.

"Just the usual."

"Trip into town went well?" Blaise couldn't help trying to find out what she'd gotten up to in town. He was getting to know Claire, and she was normally so open with what she was up to. Though, at this time of the year, maybe it was the Christmas gift shopping she was doing. Another reminder that he hadn't gotten anything for Dusty yet. It was hard to come up with an idea of what to get her when he wasn't sure what their future together was going to be.

"It did, thanks," Claire answered. She put the cream away in the fridge and packed the leftover apple pie for later.

"Coffee with the girls?" asked Blaise as he began to scrub the plates.

"Not today, I will tomorrow."

Dusty pulled the tea towel off the oven handle

and stood waiting to dry the dishes. She flicked the tea towel and said, "Come on, you're way too slow."

"I don't want to break your mom's good china."

Dusty rolled her eyes. "No, you don't."

Blaise put the first plate in the rack, he was building into a rhythm. "Just you wait, you'll be struggling to keep up."

"This isn't a race," interjected Claire with a laugh.

Blaise grinned. "I'm not competing."

He could see this as being the future with Dusty. A family. He glanced at her as she concentrated drying the plates and staking them on the kitchen table for her mom to put away.

"Like hell you aren't." Dusty flicked the towel onto his backside.

"Ow." He jumped. "That's not fair, you're distracting me."

Dusty laughed, so he grabbed a handful of bubbles and blew them on her face.

"Hey, you're playing dirty." She wiped her face with the tea towel.

"I learned from the best." He stacked the last bowl on the rack, then started on the cutlery.

Dusty winked at him.

Heat flowed through him, pushing away the hurt

at the lack of response to his question earlier about moving in. Sure, it hadn't been the best timing to ask, but he couldn't help it. He had to know. He still wanted to know. For now, though, he was content with at least getting some time with Dusty. It was good seeing her laugh—it was almost melting the tired lines away from under her eyes.

"Done." Blaise pulled the plug in the sink, then grabbed the tea towel from Dusty to wipe his hands.

"Hey." Dusty tried unsuccessfully to get it off him, her hands grabbing wildly at him.

Blaise kept turning, keeping her chasing him. "Oh, you want the tea towel back?" He stepped back, then gave it a sharp flick, snapping it on her hip.

"Ow."

It was a little too hard than he'd aimed for. "Sorry."

"Don't worry, I'll get you back." She snatched the towel from him and finished drying the last of the dishes.

Claire smiled and wiped her eyes.

"Mom, you okay?" Dusty went over to her.

"Of course, it's just... I enjoy seeing you two... you know... in love together. It makes this house feel like a home again after your dad passed."

"Oh, Mom." Dusty hugged her.

They'd been through so much and just kept going on without missing a beat. It warmed Blaise's heart to see them like this.

"Enough of that. It's time for me to go to bed." Claire patted her daughter on the shoulder and then pulled away.

"You don't have to," said Blaise. "Not on account of us." He was sure Dusty wouldn't mind him saying this. If he got to simply spend a little time with her cuddled together on the couch, then that was going to be a good way to end a long day.

"Yeah, Mom, don't go to bed on account of us."

"Don't worry, I'm not. I've got a new book I want to read."

Blaise had a sneaking feeling that wasn't the case at all. He was still very suspicious that she was up to something.

"How about you two put the Christmas tree up? It doesn't feel like Christmas without it in the living room."

"We can do that." Blaise smiled as he looked at Dusty, hoping she would agree. Despite Claire's motivations to give them space, he rather liked the idea of putting up the Christmas tree with Dusty.

"All right then, we'll put up the tree," said Dusty.

"Yes." Blaise did a little sport-like victory dance.

"You like putting up the Christmas tree or something?" Dusty asked him.

"Yeah, don't you?"

"Not really."

"Oh, but you haven't put up a Christmas tree with me before."

"Should I be worried?"

Blaise shook his head and scooped her into an embrace. "But you should be afraid."

He saw her eyes relax, then sparkle with joy. He kissed her gently on the lips.

"I'm going to bed. Night, you love birds."

Love birds? Blaise was glad they looked like a couple together.

Dusty pulled away. Her cheeks flamed red. "Night, Mom."

Blaise kept his arms around her not wanting to let go. He wasn't sure why she was embarrassed to show affection to him in front of her mom. It was only a kiss. If she'd walked in on them earlier when they were in the shed, that would've been different, of course. But here, right now, in the kitchen, this was natural, something that didn't need to be done behind closed doors.

"You embarrassed to kiss me in front of your

mom?" he asked softly when her mom had left the room.

"It's not how my family behaves."

Blaise could feel her squirming in his embrace. "What about now?" He rubbed his nose against her as if testing the waters before kissing her.

"You do like to push the boundaries." She moved her lips closer.

"You can't talk." He pressed his lips to hers, enjoying how their spirits seemed to join when they kissed. It was helping to alleviate the doubt which was building inside of him and giving him hope there would be a future together.

Dusty pulled away slowly, eyes closed as if enjoying the lingering sensation of the kiss. He enjoyed seeing the soft expression on her face.

"Let's go put up the Christmas tree?" she said.

"Where is it kept?" Dusty paused and thought. "That's right, in the garage. Come on."

Blaise followed her to the garage, the outside lights pushing away the shadows of the night which always seemed darker here in the country than in the city. A few of the cats trotted in with them to check out what was going on.

"It's on top of the cabinet..." Dusty pointed as she went to get it down. "There."

"Let me." Blaise nearly had to push her out of the way. "I want to help, you know."

Dusty stopped. Her expression a little confused. "I know."

"You don't let me, though."

"I don't mean to, it's just that I'm so used to doing things myself. It's just the way it is on the farm."

Blaise nodded. He was beginning to realize that. "Just remember, I'm here." He ran his hand down her arm.

"I will try."

It was the best answer he could've gotten from her. He reached up and shimmied the large box to the edge, then pulled it down with a little grunt. It wasn't heavy, just oversized and awkward to maneuver.

"I'll grab the decorations. They should be in a box over here." Dusty moved a couple of boxes which were stacked up along the far side of the garage wall. "Here they are."

"We're set then."

"We are."

Blaise carried the Christmas tree box back inside with Dusty following behind juggling two boxes of decorations.

"I would've guessed you'd have a real tree for

Christmas." He put the box down on the carpet in the middle of the living room and began to open it.

Dusty shrugged her shoulders. "Never had the time to bother with getting a real tree."

"Not with the harvest, I get it." He should've realized.

"Yeah, and to get the right-size pine, we'd have to go to the Adelaide Hills, which is too far away."

Blaise nodded as he pulled out the parts of the plastic Christmas tree. "This is a good one."

"We did think about getting a eucalyptus branch one year, but again, there's just not time for something like that. Hell, I haven't even done my Christmas shopping."

"What?" Blaise pretended to be surprised. "You mean to tell me you haven't bought me a gift?"

"I haven't. But I will, when the harvest is done."

"Well, I guess I should be grateful that you're going to buy me something, and that you don't think I've been too naughty to get a gift." He paused from unfolding the branches of the tree and winked at her. "I could be naughtier, though, if you like?"

She laughed and took out the gold tinsel from one of the boxes she'd carried inside. "Come here and let me wrap you then."

Blaise stepped to her. She put the tinsel around

his neck and used it to pull him to her. She kissed him, her lips setting a blazing heat on his. He moaned softly, feeling his body beginning to respond, despite the release they'd only had hours ago.

"Cool down, boy, we've got a Christmas tree to decorate," Dusty said breaking the kiss and letting the tinsel fall around him.

"I thought you wanted me to be naughtier?" He lifted an eyebrow.

She laughed. "Later."

He sighed with disappointment. "You do say that a lot, you know."

"Hey, weren't you satisfied in the shed?"

"Hmmm... well..."

Dusty playfully hit him on the arm.

"Don't hurt me." He rubbed the spot she'd hit.

"Toughen up, city boy."

"You're a hard taskmaster."

"You remember that." She pointed her finger at him, her eyes dancing with fun. He loved seeing her more relaxed, and to have this time with her was great. It was helping so much for him to think of a future with her, even if she were reluctant to let him move in.

She picked up a homemade bauble. "This is the

first one I made. I remember Mom teaching me how to thread the sequins on a pin, and then where to stick it into on the foam sphere."

"Very clever. I guess each decoration has a story?"

"They do." She stepped over the box and hung the bauble on the tree.

"I look forward to hearing about them." Blaise picked up a piece of woven wheat. "Tell me the story for this one?"

Dusty took it from him, her fingers brushed against his sending an electrifying bolt right through him.

"Mom made that for the first Christmas she and Dad had together."

He saw the emotion build in her eyes. "You miss him."

She nodded, turned her back, and hung it on the tree. Blaise moved in behind her, wrapping his arms around her. She leaned back into him, letting him support her, and he squeezed her tightly. Glad that for once, she was willing to fully open her heart to him.

Dusty patted his arm. "We should get this tree decorated."

He reluctantly let go. "We should." He bent down

and picked up a tangled string of electric lights. "Tackle this first?"

"Yes." She hated how the lights always ended up in a knotty mess. They worked together, untangling the lights and managing not to get in to an argument. Dusty hung them carefully around the branches. Then they started on placing the ornaments. Settling into a routine where Blaise would pick up a decoration and Dusty would share the story behind it as she hung it on the tree.

Blaise felt like they were finally bonding. This time together was precious, more so because he'd waited so long to get a moment where they could both be themselves together. And he was learning so much about her family through the stories of each decoration.

"Now, for the star on the top." Dusty took out the big glitter gold star from its own box. "This is what Dad got Mom the Christmas before they were married."

She went over to the tree, stood on her tippy toes trying to reach the top.

"Here." Blaise put his arms around her. "I'll lift you. Ready?"

She nodded. "Don't drop me."

"Geez, have some faith." He chuckled. He'd

learned ages ago her sense of humor was more on the sarcastic side.

"Okay... one, two, three." He lifted her from the ground, holding her tight around the waist.

"Nearly... a little to the right... no the other right... got it."

Blaise let her down a little too quickly, and she stumbled back into him but he caught her. "We're done."

She looked up at him. "You nearly dropped me."

"I contest that. Besides, I caught you easily enough." Before she could say anything else, he kissed her, dancing his lips with hers until he felt her relax into him.

"Should we turn on the Christmas tree lights?" he asked.

She stepped back. "I'll turn them on, you get the living room lights."

With a flick of the switch, Blaise plunged the room into darkness for a second before it flooded with colorful flickering lights from the tree. He smiled. "They work."

"A job well done." She slipped her arms around him, and he hugged her back.

This was turning out to be one of the best nights

together. They stood, embraced, while the lights danced to a mesmerizing rhythm.

Dusty yawned.

Blaise squeezed her tight. He'd forgotten how tired she was and the long hours she'd been working.

"Bedtime," he said softly in her ear. She nodded. He realized this would be the point when he normally would drive back to Wilkton, but he didn't want to leave her tonight.

"Can I stay the night?" The question had been burning on his lips since dinner. Sure, he'd stayed over periodically over the last year, her mom making herself scarce and subtly giving them the space they needed to get to know each other, both in and out of the bedroom. But recently, Dusty had been too busy and then too tired, and he felt that the harvest, while important for the survival of the farm, was getting between them. Even though they'd had been intimate earlier, Blaise wanted to stay the night and share a bed with the woman he loved.

"I don't think it's a good idea. I need to be up early," replied Dusty.

"Bloody hell, Dusty. Sometimes I think you really don't want to be in any sort of relationship with me."

"That's not true."

"What's wrong with me staying the night?"

"Nothing."

"You're ashamed of me?"

"No." Her answer lacked conviction. "Blaise, sorry, I'm just not used to this."

"Do you think you could be? It's been nearly a year, and sometimes I don't feel any closer to you."

"I can be."

"You sure."

She nodded. "It's just that mom's here." She lowered her voice.

"Your mom doesn't care. And it's not like anything's going to happen between us tonight other than sleeping."

She paused.

"Dusty, I'll respect whatever you decide, but think about where you'd like our relationship to go. I don't want to keep going back to my place at night, not after spending a wonderful evening with you."

"Okay."

He paused. "You mean it?"

"I do."

Blaise didn't want to push the conversation, but since he'd made a step forward, he was willing to take another chance. "I still have the unanswered question from earlier."

"What?"

"Do you think I could move in soon?" Blaise couldn't believe he'd managed to pluck up the courage to ask Dusty this, now, during harvest, when the combine was broken in the yard. And after she'd rejected the answer earlier.

Dusty turned and looked at him, her eyes clear like the summer sky. "Yes."

He detected hesitation in her voice. "I sense a but coming on."

She lowered her voice. "What about Mom?"

He nodded. "I don't expect her to move out, you know."

"You'd be happy for her to live with us?"

He wasn't sure that was the way to word it. He'd much prefer it if they had their own space, but this was a situation that wasn't the norm. Because of the attraction he had for Dusty, he was willing to compromise. It did help that he got along with Claire very well.

"This is her home."

Dusty nodded. "It's good to know that you think that way." Her smile sent a glowing warmth through him. "We can talk more later."

"Sure." He'd pushed her to face this enough for one night.

"Come on, I'm hitting the sack even though I should have a shower." She inhaled leaning toward him. "You should, too, but don't worry about it."

"Come here."

Dusty wriggled out of his grasp. "Bedtime, and no hanky-panky."

"Cross my heart." He made a cross on his heart as he said the words.

He didn't care. All he wanted was to have the night with Dusty in his arms.

CHAPTER 6

Thursday, December 19th, 2019

The sound of a magpie calling outside aroused Dusty. She carefully rolled away from Blaise, yawning the last of the sleep away, and sat on the edge of the bed. She wished she could settle back next to him and go back to sleep. She had time. It wasn't as if she could get on the combine this morning and get started reaping the last paddock of wheat. Not with it broken in the yard.

Dusty knew that if she stayed in bed with Blaise, it would only be more difficult to get up later. And since later was only in a few minutes, she figured there was no point delaying getting started for the day. Plus, she didn't want to linger in bed and have the lay-in turn into something more intimate. Not with her mom in the house.

There will be plenty of time for sleep-ins later, she thought.

Carefully, she stood so as not to wake him and glanced at Blaise sleeping in her bed, his naked chest from the sheet that covered his lower body, and his arm bent back over his head. He looked peaceful. Hot. Sexy. Desirable. The sort of man she wanted to keep in her bed. Yet, there was a niggling feeling moving inside of her, one that caused her to hesitate.

There were so many details to sort out. It wasn't as simple as him moving in. There was also her mom to consider. She wasn't about to tell her mom to go live somewhere else. *How was it really going to work with her mom living with them?* This was something she'd been putting off thinking about for the last year.

At the beginning of the year, all she wanted to know was if things could go smoothly with Blaise. It had gone better than she'd ever hoped for. Much better. What he was asking about moving in wasn't unreasonable. For whatever reason, it sent her mind blank and her stomach roiling and twisting.

She shook her head. It was too hard to think about this so early in the morning, especially when looking at Blaise mostly naked in her bed.

Dusty grabbed a fresh pair of jeans, shirt, underwear, and socks, then tiptoed out of her bedroom to the seventies-style bathroom that was long overdue for an update. There was no money to maintain the farmhouse. She and her mom had to make do, but she didn't care so much. It wasn't like she needed a fancy bathroom. This one was small, but there was a nice long bathtub and a tiny shower cubicle. It was clean, and with the water shortage they often faced, it wasn't as if she spent a lot of time in there.

Water streamed down her body washing away the grime of the past day and easing the thoughts tangling in her mind. She let her mind drift, thinking of nothing except the water running over her skin.

A soft knock on the bathroom door brought her attention back to the now.

"No need to knock, come on in." Dusty figured it was her mom, and she must need something in the bathroom.

The door opened then closed.

Dusty got on with her shower, taking out the cucumber scented shower gel and began to lather up the soap over her body.

The glass door of the shower began to slide open.

Dusty jumped. "Hey."

"I thought you said it was okay to come in," said Blaise.

She noticed how naked he was, all of him, every bit of his skin showing to her. His cock partially aroused. Her body tingled with desire as he stepped into the shower with Dusty.

"I didn't think it was you."

Water dribbled down his chest, sending her desires wild with need. There wasn't a lot of room in the small shower, forcing them to be close, and Dusty was unable to step away from him. She didn't want to. But she did hold on to a sense of propriety.

"Who the hell did you think it was, then?" He went to wrap his arms around her, but she pushed them away.

"Not now." She didn't like seeing the disappointment in his eyes. They were in a relationship, them in the shower naked should be something they did every day.

"I can help you get clean."

"I'm clean enough," she shot back as she tried to shimmy around him in the shower to wash off the soap. Moving also stopped her from gazing at his desirable body.

"Can't even tempt you with a bit of a massage?"

Her breath caught in her throat—a massage would be great. Though, they were only just in summer now, and she wasn't sure the rainwater tanks were full enough for long showers. "Can't have long showers here. Remember, this is rainwater."

He sighed deeply with frustration.

"How about back at your place," she suggested, hoping he'd see it as an alternative.

"But not until after harvest, right?"

His words squeezed her heart.

"That's right. Plus, wouldn't you rather have privacy and know that it's just you and me here."

"It's not as if your mom will find out. I can be discrete."

"This..." she waved her hands around, "... is not discrete." Dusty turned to face Blaise.

The cheeky look on his face flamed her desire toward him.

"I can tease you. With my mouth, or hands. You can choose."

Her lower abdominal muscles clenched tightly. She put her hands on his shoulder, leaned forward kissing him passionately.

"I knew I could turn you around," he mumbled, his hands moving along her wet back. His touch felt great, natural, and she wanted more. She stepped in closer to him, leaning against his wet body, feeling the heat of his skin on hers and his hardening cock pressing against her upper thigh.

She sighed, her own frustration breathing out between them. There was no way she was going to give in to her desires. Or to his request.

Fuck, it was hard.

"Oh, you wish. I wish." She pushed open the shower door.

"Hey, come back."

"I can tease, too." She shot him a cheeky glance, wriggled her hips, then shut the glass door.

"No fair."

Dusty could see him smiling at her through the glass. She was glad he was taking this well.

"Jobs won't do themselves." She grabbed her towel and began to dry off. Quickly, before she gave in to the strong urges that were thrumming through her and jumped back into the shower with Blaise to finish the teasing they'd started.

"Not on a farm."

"Or if you're running your own business."

"No."

Dusty slipped on her clothes. She paused. The last thing she wanted to be doing was to be pushing Blaise away. It wasn't really what she'd planned to do. Juggling Blaise's needs, their relationship, and the farm work with the harvest was trickier than she thought.

"Harvest will be finished soon."

"I know. But then it will be another job which will have your attention."

He had a point. *Could she change?* Find a way to make time to give to Blaise. Time which he more than deserved as her boyfriend.

There was one obvious way for that to happen— have him move in.

Her stomach fluttered with nerves. She could think better once the crops were reaped.

"I'll go ring Bluey and see if he can come out this morning. I'm sure he can fix the combine. Then as long as the weather doesn't get too hot, the harvest should be finished. Then we can finish this conversation."

It was the best she could do.

Even for her, she knew that wasn't enough.

BLAISE RESTED his forehead on the cool glass of the shower. The sound of the bathroom door closing jarring to hear. He'd taken a risk to come into the shower like he had. It hadn't quite played out the way he'd wanted it to.

A hint of rejection welled inside of him. Blaise had a flashing thought of giving up and going back to Adelaide. Then he inhaled, and the childish thought dissipated as quickly as it had come.

Blaise knew what he was getting into when starting a relationship with Dusty and how she'd been hurt by Aaron. The running of the farm was her business, and like many jobs, it was her life. He liked that. She was dedicated, a hard worker, and most of all, sassy.

She did let me stay overnight, he reminded himself.

That was a big step for Dusty. She was trying. More than that, her action gave him the hope he needed right now. He had to keep the bigger picture in mind. He'd been here for nearly a year and known Dusty for nearly two. He wasn't about to walk away from her, not when there was a glimmer of change she'd shown. Besides, he'd come into the shower full well knowing that it would stir her up.

He couldn't resist the temptation when he'd woken to an empty bed, then discovered she was in the shower.

He grinned to himself as he took out the soap. It had been a bit of fun.

She can handle it.

Blaise finished in the shower and turned off the water, not wanting to run the tanks low and give Dusty a reason to be cranky at him. Not when things were starting to change in a way that Blaise had been hoping would happen for so long.

THE DAY WAS ALREADY WARMING, and it wasn't even nine in the morning. The sun's rays radiated strong heat with no traces of clouds in the sky reflecting off the galvanized iron sheds, intensifying the heat around them. Dust hung heavy on the air. There'd already been no rain for the month of December, and there wasn't likely to be much now until next year. The flat landscape revealed a hundred different shades of brown. The only bit of green in sight was some grass growing at the bottom of the tap by the shed.

Molly sat on the back of Dusty's ute in the shed,

looking with hope in her eyes that maybe this was the day she would get to do some sheep work. Ted laid in the shade under Bluey's ute, stretched out, head resting on his front paws as he pretended to sleep but keeping one eye on the activities in the yard.

Dusty stood nervously watching the mechanic, Bluey, who had come out especially as a favor. He was quiet and hadn't said a word for the last ten minutes as he looked over the combine. Dusty bit her bottom lip, not wanting to say anything. She was hoping against the nervous knots forming in her stomach that this wasn't a bad breakdown of machinery, or that it wasn't going to cost more than she could afford, and that it could be fixed, preferably within an hour.

Blaise stood by her side, hands in his pocket. She wanted to lean into him. Take some of the calm and strength that exuberated from him. She looked at him out of the corner of her eye. He was wearing the same clothes as yesterday but now a little dirty and crumpled.

Dusty blushed as she remembered what they had got up to in the shed. Then the bit of fun in the shower this morning. The cheekiness of Blaise kept her on her toes. While at times she found it hard sharing her life with him, at the moment she was glad he'd stayed over. He had a way of getting under her skin, of getting her riled up, which her instinct was then to push him away when that wasn't really what she wanted to do. She needed to come up with a way forward with him or lose him forever. He was getting impatient and rightly so. It's just that she didn't want to feel pressured. She needed to be sure.

A ute rattled down the driveway.

Dusty watched to see who the hell might be coming here today. She wasn't expecting anyone. Her mouth dried when she realized it was Aaron's ute.

What the hell does he want?

Aaron parked his ute, got out, and sauntered over to them. "Saw your ute from the road, Bluey. Thought I'd drop in. Need any help?" He grinned sideways at Dusty. She shivered despite the warming heat of the day.

Dusty shrugged her shoulders and looked away, her blood beginning to boil merely from his presence. Aaron was a nosy shit. Coming in here to gloat at her for having machinery issues so close to the end of harvest, she just knew it. After all that had gone on between him and her, he was always going to be a burr in her side. He didn't take rejection well, especially when she'd chosen a city boy as a boyfriend over him.

"We're good," interrupted Blaise.

"Lucky I came along and helped your boyfriend yesterday with a flat tire. He was in a right pickle." Aaron ignored Blaise and kept talking.

"I could've handled it." Blaise changed his stance, putting his hands on his hips, his glare at Aaron was stormy.

Aaron chuckled. "Yeah, right."

"What do you want, Aaron?" Dusty was trying to think quickly. At this rate, Blaise and Aaron would come to fisticuffs.

"I'm a friendly neighbor checking in to make sure you're all right and don't need any help."

Dusty was about to say she didn't need any help, and most definitely didn't need it from him, her ex who had hit her, who had nearly cost her and Blaise starting a relationship together, when Bluey cleared this throat, steeping around from behind the combine.

"You're not going to like what I have to say." He ran his hand through his dark hair.

Dusty felt her breath leave her, squashing her lungs. "No?"

"You're right, it's a broken bearing."

Fuck. She forced herself to take a breath.

"You can fix it?" she asked.

"Yep, but I have to order the part from Melbourne. I have none in stock."

"Fuck it!" This time Dusty swore out loud. Her mind whirled. Today was Thursday. With Christmas Day next Wednesday, it meant it would be cutting it too fine for the part to arrive in time. *I won't get the harvest done before Christmas.*

She felt Blaise move to stand close to her, his hand on the small of her back, quietly offering support.

"Sorry, I wish I had better news. With Christmas next week, things are getting tight."

Dusty nodded. There was no point getting angry at Bluey. She'd had hoped that the harvest would be done, then she would be able to focus on her relationship with Blaise. The breakdown of the combine was putting this all at risk.

She scuffed her boots in the dirt trying to think —there was one possibility.

"What if I drive to get the part myself? Would

you install the new bearing for me, even if it's the weekend?"

Bluey rubbed his scruffy chin in thought. It was a busy time of year for him too with the farmers needing machinery fixed and not wanting to wait.

"I figure I can leave straight away. If I push it, I'll get to the store before closing tonight, then I'll turn around and come straight back. All being well, I'll have the part tomorrow."

"You can't drive like that," said Blaise.

She ignored the look of concern on his face. This is what needed to be done to finish the harvest, to ensure that she had income for the year ahead, and so she could be present for her and Blaise's first Christmas together.

"You'll be lucky to get there before the shop closes." Bluey shook his head. "Blaise is right. It's dangerous to drive like that. You will need to rest. It's not worth the trip if you end up dead on the side of the road."

Dusty felt a chill from his words. She knew the risk. Dammit! Right now, she was willing to take it. There was a lot riding on this. It wasn't just a matter of finishing the harvest before Christmas, it was the future of her farm, and it was the future with Blaise. She wasn't going to give up on either of those.

"How about I go with you," spoke up Aaron.

"No way, if anyone's going with Dusty, it will be me." Blaise turned to Dusty. "We can share the driving."

That would be a much better option than driving with Aaron. "You have time?" She wasn't sure what his schedule was like with his accounting business. She'd been so wrapped up in the harvest that she'd lost touch in what he was doing.

"Of course."

It was going to be a big drive. She was used to the long hours behind the wheel, but Aaron wasn't. She rolled her lips in thought.

"Better to go with someone, Dusty," piped up Bluey. "That reminds me, I've got your tire fixed, you'll need the space with you."

Dusty nodded. And that someone was most definitely Blaise. She was about to turn down Aaron when she noticed her mom rushing toward them. She could tell straight away something was wrong.

"Mom, what's happened?" She braced herself for more bad news.

"Blaise, you need to go back to Adelaide. Your dad's been in an accident."

BLAISE FELT like someone had punched him hard in the stomach and the wind rushed from his lungs.

"What happened?" asked Blaise. He could feel the blood draining from his face, and his head felt light with the abrupt news. "Is he okay?"

Claire's face creased with concern. "Last night, he had an accident at an intersection. His car was written off. He spent the night in intensive care."

"Bloody hell." Blaise breathed out heavily. "Why wasn't I told sooner?"

"I don't know, I guess your mom and Scott were in shock. He's in the Royal Adelaide Hospital."

"I'll go there straight away." He wished he had a change of clothes, but there was no way he was about to lose an hour or so driving back into Wilkton to change. He was going to drive straight back to Adelaide now. He had to see his dad.

Blaise paused, his mind catching up to process everything that was happening right now. Of course, he was going to rush to see his dad, but where did that leave Dusty. She needed that part for the combine. There was no way she could drive all that way by herself and back again. It was a nine-hour trip one way. The last thing he wanted to hear was that she'd been in an accident too.

"Don't worry about me," said Dusty as if reading

what he was thinking. "I'll get the part, or harvest will just have to wait this time."

"I can go with you," said Aaron. "I mean it with my offer. A neighborly gesture."

Blaise narrowed his eyes at Aaron. He didn't trust him. Not one bit.

"I'm not sure what you're discussing, but you know I can help," said Claire.

Blaise knew Claire was strong for her age, but he didn't like the idea of her driving long hours either. He itched to get on the road back to Adelaide, but he was going nowhere until he knew what Dusty had decided.

"What are neighbors for in times like this?" Aaron said.

Dusty sighed heavily. "Fine."

"No." Blaise's eyes widened. There was no way he was going to let this happen. The problem was, right now, it was obvious he couldn't stop it.

Fuck it.

"Don't worry, Blaise, I'll take good care of Dusty." Aaron smirked.

Blaise took a deep breath. He looked at Dusty. This was going to be a test between them. He was going to have to trust that she could handle herself with Aaron for the next twenty-four to thirty hours.

His gut twisted painfully. The idea of them spending so much time together, just them, sent him on edge.

"Blaise, go be with your dad. I'll see you when I get back," said Dusty firmly. She stepped up and put her hands on his shoulders and gazed into his eyes. He desperately looked for some reassurance but didn't find enough.

"Trust me, I can handle him. There will be no time for anything to happen. We both have to focus on driving," she spoke softly so only he could hear.

Blaise hated how he didn't have a choice in this situation.

Dusty kissed him. He barely felt her touch or the connection of their souls as their lips touched. He yearned to be with her fully without these problems getting in the way.

"I'll be fine. You go to your dad."

Blaise looked into her eyes, they were defiant, determined. He knew it didn't matter how much he protested this situation, Dusty was going to drive to Melbourne with Aaron to get the part. And he was going to drive to Adelaide to see if his dad was all right.

What scared the hell out of him was how this was going to impact their relationship.

When he saw her next, was she going to still

want him or would Aaron have gotten to her? It was a leap of faith he was being forced to take, which he didn't want to. A test of their relationship.

With a gut-wrenching twist, he knew he was going to have to let things unfold and hope that what they had together was going to be enough.

CHAPTER 7

"Don't think that this means anything," said Dusty as she started her ute, revving the engine into action.

Aaron sat in the passenger seat, the gearstick the only thing between them in the cab of the ute. She hated being so close to this man. He'd hurt her deeply, but right now, she had no choice.

In a way, it was sort of acceptable. After all, this is what neighbors did in the country—put aside their differences and helped each other. Her stomach tightened as she drove down the driveway away from Acacia Plains. How she wished it was someone else helping her.

"Wouldn't think otherwise," answered Aaron, his tone suggesting otherwise.

"I think it best we drive in silence." Dusty pressed heavily on the accelerator. She wanted this trip with Aaron over as soon as possible.

"Killjoy."

Dusty pursed her lips together. They had the next nine hours together, and her focus was to arrive safely and before closing time. Not talking to Aaron to pass the time was also high on her list.

"Your mom packed a good stash of food for us."

Dusty heard Aaron rustling through the esky by his feet.

"Don't start eating now, it's too early in the trip." She gripped her hands tightly on the steering wheel as she turned onto the highway. Her mom was good at packing comfort food. It hadn't taken her long to put together an esky of food for them.

Though it had taken longer to get on the road than she would've liked. Aaron needed to go back to his place and sort out a few things.

Blaise had gotten into his car straight away, leaving Dusty to make sure that things were as easy as possible for the evening jobs for her mom to do. It was probably a good thing that her mom was staying on the farm for that reason. Dusty could tell her mom didn't approve of Aaron helping. They had a history which everyone knew about. It was risky spending time alone with him. She figured it was going to happen sometime, they were neighbors after all, and they might have miles stretching out between them, but at the end of the day, they were going to see each other.

Best to get the awkward stage over and done with.

"Think you can make it to Ballarat before I drive? Or do you want me to drive sooner?" asked Aaron as he secured the lid back on the esky and settling back into the seat.

"I can make it to Ballarat." She glanced at the fuel gauge. They were going to have to stop for fuel which was a good thing. She would need a pit stop herself, and a fresh cup of coffee. She doubted the flask of coffee her mom packed was going to last long.

The one good thing about this arrangement was that she knew Aaron would drive safely, and he was used to the open road. Blaise wasn't. She glanced at her cell attached to the bracket by the steering wheel. There were no messages, of course. She would've heard if there had been. It wasn't as if Blaise could ring or message anyway, he was driving to Adelaide. It would take him about two hours, and that's how long she was going to have to wait until hearing from him. She hoped everything was fine with his dad.

Blaise looked like he was about to explode with anger when it was suggested that Aaron drive with her to Melbourne.

When she kissed him goodbye, she saw the fear in his eyes.

Did he trust me? She clenched her jaw as she increased her speed, rattling down the highway. It might be more about Aaron, but there was a niggle that maybe he didn't trust her fully. And she only had herself to blame with the kiss Aaron forced on her. Sure, she had kissed back, but immediately regretted it. She hoped this time Aaron would keep his hands to himself.

"So how are things between you and the city boy?"

Dusty suppressed a groan of frustration.

She reached over and turned on the radio, setting the volume to high.

This was going to be a longer trip than she'd been anticipating.

***

. . .

BLAISE DROVE AS FAST as he could on the highway toward Adelaide, going further south than the direction Dusty was taking to get to Melbourne. As tempting as it was, he kept to the speed limit. He set the radio loud to help keep his concentration and resisted the urge to stop off to get a large coffee at the Wakefield service station.

He suddenly made a connection. Of course, he could stop. He didn't want to waste time at the moment, but he could feel the anxiety knotting in his belly of how he needed to see his dad sooner than later. And taking time to get a coffee which would barely take fifteen minutes wouldn't matter in the greater scheme of things.

This was how Dusty approached the harvest. No wonder she was desperate to get it done and was using Christmas as a motivator. Sure, the longer it took, the more likely the crop would be damaged. There was more to it all. For the first time, he really deeply understood her motivations and why she was rushing all the time and keeping him at arm's length.

When he was in cell range, he used his hands-free headphones to call and talk to his mom. She was upset, tired, but assured him that his dad would be fine, and if he was too busy, he didn't have to come. That she'd only rung Dusty's mom as she wanted to tell him about what had happened. There was no reason to worry, and he didn't need to come. She'd rather he stayed helping Dusty on the farm. There was no way he was turning back. He didn't think he was being told everything.

A phone call to his brother, Scott, confirmed what he'd been suspecting. Scott told him that his mom was overreacting and that everything was under control. His dad was fine, simply needed to spend a few days in hospital. Scott was managing *Blackbirds*, the pub his dad owned just fine, even with the Christmas rush.

He didn't believe them. Not everything was all right, and they were definitely keeping him in the dark.

Blaise scanned the signs at the hospital parking for directions on where to go. He found the parking entrance, powered down his window to grab a ticket from the machine and drove in. Fortunately, he found a parking space without having to do countless laps looking for one, got out, and negotiated the maze of the hospital to find his dad in the Critical Care Ward. That, in itself, wasn't a good sign. It told him that his dad had done some serious damage to himself.

He stopped to ask where his dad was at the

nurse's station. She showed him to bed number three along the corridor, and she pulled back the curtain to let Blaise in.

Blaise held his breath. *Fucking hell.*

He couldn't help it.

His dad lay in the bed, two legs in casts, and an arm in a cast too. His mom sitting on the other side of the bed looking stressed. His brother stood at the foot of the bed with shadows of tiredness under his eyes.

"Nothing serious, hey?" He raised his eyebrows questioningly at his mom.

"You came. Thank you." His mom stood, shuffled down to the end of the bed, arms out to embrace him. Blaise hugged her back.

"What happened?"

"A car turned unexpectedly hitting your dad's car."

"And you didn't think to tell me he's broken both legs?"

"One's just a fracture," his brother piped up.

"And that makes it better, how?"

"Don't get upset. I know it must be a shock. Your dad was in surgery last night. We've been here since the ambulance brought him in," said his mom.

Blaise couldn't believe it. "He's lucky."

"Very lucky."

"How long will he be in hospital?"

"The doctor has promised me he will be home for Christmas."

"I'll sit with him. How about you two go home and get some rest."

"I don't know..." His mom looked worried.

"Mom, is he stable?"

She nodded. "They're going to move him to high dependency soon."

"When they've done that, promise me you'll go home. Scott will take you." He looked at his brother, who nodded in agreement.

His mom patted him on the shoulder. "I feel bad taking you away from Dusty."

"She understands." The words came out tightly.

Dusty was genuinely concerned for his dad, and him, but he remembered she was driving to Melbourne with a man he didn't trust, and he was acutely aware of how things could end up changing because of it.

***

.   .   .

AARON PARKED the ute in the empty car park of the mechanical store, an oversized shed, on the outskirts of Melbourne.

"Fuck." Dusty could clearly see the closed sign as she peered through the windscreen. They had come all this way to save time, and now the shop was closed. She unbuckled her seatbelt, got out, and went to the door. She cupped her hands to look inside. There were no signs of anyone. In frustration, she banged on the door. This can't be happening. She'd just endured nearly eight hours of traveling in the ute with Aaron with the hope of being able to turn back and go home, only to find they were going to have to wait until morning.

"Is anyone there?" called out Aaron.

Dusty blinked back tears of frustration, then turned to go back to the ute. "No." Her shoulders slumped forward as she slid back inside.

She glanced at her phone. Minutes. They'd missed the closing time by minutes.

"It was all thanks to that bloody truck going slow," grumbled Dusty. They'd gotten stuck behind a heavy truck just out of Ballarat, and unable to overtake safely, they'd slowed down, wasting valuable time.

"Want to get a hotel room?"

Dusty glared at Aaron. "Separate rooms."

"You paying?" He raised an eyebrow.

She pressed her lips together hard. "Separate beds then."

"I think we passed one a few minutes ago that had a vacancy sign, should we try that one?"

"Good as any, I guess." She was dark at having to spend money she didn't have on a room for the night, but also dreaded how the hell she was going to tell Blaise about sharing a room with Aaron. She'd rather risk spending the night sleeping in the ute.

"You don't have to tell Blaise. I'll keep it a secret." Aaron steered the ute back onto the main road, along the way they had come.

"This isn't a situation which is secret." His comment irked her. Aaron was an opportunist, and this was going to be a long night that she could well do without.

He parked the ute at the reception area at the hotel. It looked dark and dingy. "Maybe we won't eat here," he suggested.

She was going to agree to that. "Take away sounds like a good idea."

They got out of ute. It felt weird to Dusty to lock the door before walking into reception. That was something she only ever did when in the big cities.

A large man at the desk greeted them with a smirk on his face. His blue T-shirt was dirty and worn, faded with too many washes, and tattoos flowed over his arms. The place stank of stale cigarettes and beer. This was the last place she wanted to stay.

"Room for a few hours?"

"The whole night," said Dusty.

He raised an eyebrow. "$250."

She gulped. That was way too much. Her budget was going to have to be cut back dramatically with the very expensive new bearing she had to buy for the harvester.

"Twin share," she added.

"Only got a queen size available."

Of course, she thought to herself. Things were getting worse instead of better. She felt her cell vibrate in her pocket, and she took it out.

She smiled. It was Blaise. "I gotta take this," she said quickly to Aaron, then she slipped outside to finally talk to Blaise. "How's your dad?" she asked as she accepted the call on her cell.

"Banged up pretty bad. Both legs and one arm broken. He was in surgery last night, and a bit of concussion."

"Far out."

"Yeah, he'll be all right, though. What about you? Got the… what was it again?"

"Bearing." She inhaled slowly, it was better to confess straight up. He'd find out anyway. Aaron would make sure of that.

"That's right, the bearing. On your way back?"

"Slight problem."

"Oh?"

"The store's closed. We have to wait until morning before we can get the bearing."

The silence from Blaise unnerved her.

"We're getting a hotel room, so we can rest up, sleep before the trip back tomorrow. Got no choice really." She blurted the words out before she lost her courage.

"I see." His words were sharp.

Dusty could tell from his tone he wasn't at all happy to hear what she was saying.

"Separate rooms, then?"

She swallowed hard. Looked through the reception glass door. Aaron finished talking to the man, picked up a key and turned around. He smiled at her. Dusty shivered. Aaron strode through the door to her.

"Got us a double bed for $200, thought you'd like to save a bit of money." He grinned at her.

Dusty felt her blood chill.

"What the hell, Dusty?" said Blaise.

She put the phone to her ear. "Don't worry, you can trust me. Nothing will happen. It's just unfortunate the store was closed, and that there's not a lot of cheap options for accommodations out this side of town."

"I'll pay, then you can have a room of your own. Don't worry about the money."

"Don't worry, city boy, I'll take care of Dusty better than you could. This place is better than you think."

"Fuck off, Aaron, don't you bloody touch Dusty, or I'll beat the shit out of you."

"Blaise," Dusty scrambled to think of something to help cool Blaise down. "I'm exhausted. I need sleep. It's probably better this way so we drive home safely."

"Get separate rooms," he yelled.

"Too late. It's all paid for, my shout."

"Fuck you," Blaise swore.

Dusty looked at Aaron. Whatever he was thinking, it wasn't going to happen. "I'll sleep in the ute."

"Too dangerous, you don't know who will approach you around here. Come on, best we find somewhere to eat, you can shower first if you like."

He smiled broadly at Dusty. "I'll even let you choose what side of the bed you want to sleep on."

"You better hope there's a couch, otherwise you're sleeping on the floor," said Dusty firmly.

"Dusty, I can wire through some money. You don't have to—"

"Blaise, I need you to trust me on this one. Nothing will happen between us. I love you." Then before the argument could continue, she hung up. She glared at Aaron, then realized what she'd said to Blaise. If felt right. The 'I love you' felt right, which was saying something because this situation with Aaron wasn't.

"I mean it, Aaron, you're on the couch or floor, or I get into the ute and drive away leaving you to make your own way back to your farm."

"Fine. You just remember, I'm trying to help here."

"Booking a room where we share a bed isn't helping."

"Fussy."

She glared at him. He was a tough nut to get through to. She'd faced him once before, and sure as hell she would do so again. "I'll remind you in another way then?" She held up her fist.

"Okay, okay, settle down. I'll sleep on the couch.

You remember I was trying to save money. You've got a new bearing to pay for, and they aren't cheap, you know."

Dusty didn't need to be reminded of that. New bearings were thousands and thousands of dollars. It was going to hurt. Not as much as losing Blaise because of Aaron's interfering behavior would, though.

She snatched the keys from him. Room number five. She saw the number on the door up ahead. "Neighborly help doesn't extend to physical activities of any kind, remember." Her words were sharp and to the point.

She saw the surprise in his eyes and hoped she was finally getting through to him.

CHAPTER 8

Friday, December 20th, 2019

"I'm going to be fine." His dad told him for the second time since morning tea. "You should go back to Dusty."

Blaise wanted to. He was desperate to see Dusty. *Would Aaron have gotten to her? Convinced her to go back to him?* The bastard would've tried, persistently, to bring Dusty around to having a relationship with him. He tried to take comfort in how she'd told him she loved him. *I love you.* The words had kept him up all night. He mulled over her tone, wondering if she meant those words or not. It was hard to think this was a step in the right direction when they were sharing a hotel room together, and bloody hell even a bed. *How could this have happened?*

"Blaise?" His dad interrupted his thoughts.

"I want to be here for you and mom." He wriggled on the uncomfortable chair in the room. His mom was home resting after the long hours in the hospital, and Scott was off working.

"She'll be happy to see you after her long trip."

Blaise had filled him in on what Dusty was doing. He wanted to think Dusty would be wanting to see him, but there were a few things in their way. The broken combine. The harvest. Aaron. Then there was the fact that they had been delayed a day. He flexed his hands at the thought as if he were itching to punch Aaron. He was sure that bastard was up to something. He wouldn't miss an opportunity. Dusty had tried to reassure him, but the delay was the last straw.

Do I trust her? He sort of did. Well, until finding out she was sharing a bed with Aaron last night didn't help. There had been the time when she had kissed him back. They'd worked through that, and these last few months they had put that behind them. So, he had thought.

The one thing he was clear about was not trusting Aaron.

"I dunno, she's pretty busy with the harvest." He didn't think that there was any point to rush back. Despite what his imagination was conjuring about what could've happened between Dusty and Aaron, if nothing had, if she was still interested in him, but her focus was going to be on the harvest. It was as if Dusty driving off with Aaron had ignited all his fears about their relationship.

"You can't develop the relationship here. You need to be close to her," his dad said. "Your mom is fine, Scott's looking after her. And I'll be home in a few days before Christmas."

"I'll come back for Christmas to be with you all," he said hurriedly. He didn't care what Dusty might have in mind, he was going to be with his family since she had the farm business to contend with. If by some miracle she'd finished the harvest, then she could choose to come with him or not. And if the latter, then they were going to have to have the hard conversation about the lack of future between them. *Would it come to that?* He still hoped it wouldn't. It was simply hard not to, especially when Dusty was driving with Aaron somewhere between Melbourne and Acacia Plains. The fear played too heavily on his imagination, and he couldn't shake the doubt.

"I think you should have it with Dusty. It will be

your first Christmas together, after all. Your mom will understand, you know."

"I don't want to disappoint her."

"You would disappoint her more if you upset Dusty, ended up single, and put the chance of her having grandkids off even longer."

That sounded about right to Blaise. His mom didn't openly say much about how she was looking forward to being a grandma, but there'd been a few comments in the last year which he could recall suggesting that she was excited about the prospect.

"So, what do you say?"

"How about I stay today and go back tomorrow," suggested Blaise.

"You should be there when she gets back. It will let her know you're there for her."

"You're sounding like Mom." Blaise rested his head into his hand. His dad did have a good point. His mind might be going crazy with what could potentially be happening between Dusty and Aaron, but he still had feelings for her. Strong enough feelings to have Dusty in his future. By being back at the farm, that was more likely to happen. They couldn't develop their relationship if they were apart.

His dad chuckled then groaned in pain. "Hurts to laugh."

"Are you sure you don't want me to stay longer?"

"Positive. Your mom would never forgive me if she thought I was keeping you and Dusty apart."

"You're doing nothing of the sort."

"Then you will have Christmas with her."

Blaise nodded. "I'll come have Christmas dinner with you."

"On Boxing Day, and you can only come if you bring Dusty."

"You've been spending way too much time with Mom, haven't you? That's exactly something she would say."

"Let me tell you a secret. It's important to make sure your wife is happy. And I know that this is what will make your mom happy."

Blaise smiled. His dad might be in the hospital in pain, but his sense of humor was still coming through. "I'm starting to think that you'd rather Dusty come for Christmas instead of me."

"We want the complete package, son." His dad sighed.

Blaise could tell his dad was getting tired. "I'll let you have a rest."

"Not yet. First you need to show me those photos of the combine you've been driving. I need to believe that my accountant son has been getting his hands dirty."

"Gee, thanks, Dad," said Blaise sarcastically as he took out his cell. The first thing he noticed was there were no messages from Dusty. It wasn't easy not knowing. He vaguely remembered Claire telling him that this was the way it was often on the farm. *Could I get used to this?* He flicked through the pictures to the one where he was standing near the combine and showed his dad.

His dad whistled. "Big, eh?"

"Yeah, and I couldn't believe how tired I was after driving it for only a short time."

Blaise flicked through a few more photographs from the farm, noticing that his dad was getting more and more sleepy.

"I'll go now. Rest up, Dad."

His dad nodded and closed his eyes. "Looking forward to seeing you and Dusty together."

Blaise hoped so too.

DUSTY AND AARON stopped at a service station to refuel the ute and get some food. To have a break from sitting, they stood by the ute, eating their burgers. They were four hours away from arriving at Acaia Plains.

Dusty rolled up the paper and threw it in the bin. "That was deliciously disgusting."

Aaron chuckled. "It was." He licked the barbecue sauce from his fingers.

"I can't wait to sleep in my own bed tonight," said Dusty.

"I could join you?"

"Like hell. How many times do I need to tell you no?"

"The way I see it is that I've now got leverage, so maybe you need to reassess things."

"What do you mean?"

"I can tell your city boyfriend that, you know… you just couldn't resist me."

"That's a lie."

"He won't know that." Aaron smirked.

How dare he.

"I thought you were being neighborly? Turns out that really isn't in your nature."

He stepped toward her, arms out, trying to embrace Dusty. "You just need convincing of who is the real man you should choose."

Dusty kicked him. Hard. In the balls.

Aaron doubled over, gasping in pain.

"I have chosen the real man. Now, he will believe me because, let's just say, you're going to be walking as if injured, and Blaise will believe me that I kicked you right where it hurts."

Aaron stared blankly at Dusty. It was her turn to smirk. She'd got him. Messed up his plans.

"You've got three seconds to get in the ute, or I'm leaving you behind." She walked around the ute, and got in, starting it up.

Aaron limped into the passenger's seat. He didn't say a word.

Dusty felt a surge of confidence go through her. She'd chosen her man, and now it was time to make sure that he was going to be around for the future.

That's if she hadn't left it too late.

CHAPTER 9

Blaise turned from the dirt road into Acacia Plains driveway. He'd slept in his old room in his parents' house last night. The noise of the city kept him awake for hours. He couldn't wait to get back to the quiet of his rental in Wilkton. His dad was still in the hospital. It would take a while before he was back on his feet, and then walking again as his broken legs healed. His dad was alive and would be fine. Blaise took a punt and told them he and Dusty would be down Christmas evening.

Fuck, he hoped that would happen.

It was as if saying that to them would help it to come true. Then he had no idea what could go on in her mind during the trip to and from Melbourne with Aaron. The whole sharing the same room left him unsettled. He had some way of getting under her skin. *Would Aaron manage to again?*

I can trust her. He knew that, but he wanted to see her to be sure.

Blaise slowed down looking ahead at the combine. There was no activity. No Dusty. Bluey wasn't there either. It was late morning. It was meant to be a trip there and back. Overnight. It worried him that she'd be too tired to keep driving, and after his dad being in a car accident, his stomach had been roiling with worry. The road to Melbourne was notorious in parts for high-speed accidents.

Could that have happened to Dusty?

Is that why there was no sign of her now?

Blaise parked his Audi car near the back gate of the farmhouse, got out his phone and checked it. There were no messages from Dusty. No calls. Nothing. His gut tightened with worry. *Had something bad happened?*

Ted came up to greet him as he got out of the car.

"Good boy. Where's Dusty, hey?" He patted the kelpie behind the ears before walking into the house yard.

"Dusty? Claire? Anyone home?" Blaise had

learned quickly that calling out was the best way to get their attention.

No one answered. He knocked on the back door, then checked if it was locked. It wasn't. He pushed the door open.

"You there, Claire?" he yelled out.

"In the kitchen, Blaise."

He breathed out with relief. Glad that someone was home.

"Is Dusty back?"

"Not yet. Have you heard from her?" She was at the kettle, two cups ready. "Tea?"

"Thanks." He plonked onto one of the kitchen chairs at the table. It was Claire's pastime to make everyone a cup of tea. Right now, he could do with one.

"I haven't heard from her. You?"

"Not this morning." She turned from the kettle, two cups in hand. "I'm sure she's fine. She was when she rang me a few hours ago."

"They got the part then?"

"Yes." She set a cup of tea in front of Blaise, then sat opposite him. She seemed distracted. Her eyes reflected a dark shadow of worry.

He hated that Dusty and Aaron shared a room at

a hotel. Sure, he wanted Dusty to drive safely. But had it ended up as something more?

If only I could've gone instead.

"Oh, look at me, how could I forget. We need some cake. I made some last night." Claire got up from her chair and went over to the counter area. "Jubilee cake, which I think now is one of your favorites?"

"Only if you've made it." He'd first tasted a Jubilee cake nearly two years ago when he first came to Wilkton as part of his job as an accountant. The cake had sultanas and raisins it in, and tasted delicious fresh with butter smeared on a slice.

Claire placed a plate of sliced cake on the table, then took out the butter from the fridge. "Argh, I'm forgetful today. Let me get some plates."

"I should ring Dusty." Blaise got out his phone. He couldn't blame her for being absent-minded with Dusty not being back, but the call went straight to voice mail. *Dammit.*

Blaise put his phone on the table. "Maybe she's out of cell phone range."

"You sort of get used to being kept in the dark like this. My husband would be gone for hours and hours working on the farm."

"I can't stand waiting."

"Though, I must say, having cell phones has helped." She looked at him. "That's when they answer or are in range or haven't gone flat."

Blaise harrumphed.

"I need your help with something." Claire turned the cup of tea around on the kitchen table.

"Of course, what would you like me to do?" Blaise needed something to take his mind off the fact that Dusty was driving with Aaron, and they should've been back by now.

"You need to keep a secret from Dusty."

"You sure that's a good idea?" Last time he'd gone behind Dusty's back and helped Claire by going through the farm's accounts, it had tested her patience, to say the least.

Claire waved her hand in a dismissive gesture. "Don't worry about her. She'll be fine."

Blaise couldn't be sure. Too much had happened in the lead-up to Christmas, and he wasn't sure she'd come back wanting to be with him. The time he had with his family in the city reinforced he wanted to move here and live with Dusty, but he wasn't going to wait around for her to make up her mind.

He was sure what he wanted.

Her.

Forever.

If she couldn't make up her mind, then he couldn't help thinking that it would mean their future was going to be rocky, and the lack of commitment from Dusty was going to push him away.

That, in itself, was telling him that their future wasn't likely to be together. Christmas or not, the direction of their relationship had reached a critical point.

"She won't take any of Aaron's lip, so stop worrying."

Blaise glanced at Claire. He didn't really want to tell her what he was really considering—to stay or to head back to Adelaide.

The lights of the Christmas tree caught his eye. It had been a genuinely fun night when they'd decorated the tree. It felt like he was beginning to make his own family with Dusty as they hung the ornaments.

Why did relationships always seem to get rocky near Christmas?

"I know... well, I know you two need some privacy."

"Claire, don't worry, I'm not moving in." He couldn't hide the bitter tone from his voice.

"Don't be so sure about that." Her voice took on a motherly tone of 'I know better.'

He shrugged his shoulders. What she did say was true. He wasn't sure of that. And it was tearing him up inside. That, and she was driving hundreds of miles with that bastard Aaron. *Who knew what could happen?* Dusty had almost gone back to him just after he'd met her two years ago, even after Aaron had hit her.

"Will you help me?" Claire asked again.

"What do you want to do?"

Claire smiled. "I'm moving out."

"You're what?" Blaise nearly spilled his tea.

She looked very proud of herself. "I'm moving out. I've bought a unit in the retirement village."

"What? Why?" His mind was racing—this was Claire's home here on Acacia Plains.

"Because you two need your space."

"You're jumping ahead a bit, I haven't moved in, and I'm not sure Dusty will ever agree that I can."

"That's why I've bought the unit. It's part of my plan to get out of the way of being an excuse for her to stop you from moving in."

"You don't have to move out on account of me." He ran his hand through his hair.

He'd never really thought that Claire would have to move out if he came to Acacia Plains to live. He wasn't sure how Dusty was going to take this news when she got back either. His stomach churned with worry that she would blame him for Claire moving out.

"I do." She leaned over the kitchen table and patted him on the arm. "I want you as a son-in-law, you know, and I do know my daughter."

Blaise wasn't sure what to say about all of this. Claire seemed to have a bit more of an idea of what was going on with Dusty than he'd thought possible.

"She just needs a little push."

"I don't think Dusty likes being pushed."

"No. But doesn't mean they're not good for her. Now, are you going to help me get a few things moved in?"

"It won't be the same not having you around here."

"I'll come visit."

Blaise chuckled. "How are we going to keep this a secret?"

"She's going to be too busy over the next few days getting the harvest finished."

"You've thought about this too much."

"I have." Claire looked proud of her efforts.

"Then I'm in."

Dusty fought against the urge to speed down the driveway of Acacia Plains. The last part of the trip with Aaron had been in awkward silence, but she didn't care. He'd done the neighborly thing to help, but his true nature still showed its ugly self.

She'd spent the last few hours worrying about Blaise, and if he were even going to be around. She deliberately hadn't called or messaged him. They needed to speak in person. It had been hard to resist contacting him. What helped keep her steady in her decision was that she didn't want Aaron to overhear the conversation or read a text message. The last half hour felt like forever as she sped toward Acacia Plains.

Dusty hoped that Blaise would be there, so they could talk.

She parked the ute at the back of the house.

"You can go home now. Thanks for your help." She paused. "You get that I will never choose you."

Aaron glared at her then gave a slight nod of his head.

"Don't bloody forget it."

Dusty opened the driver's door and got out. Ted rushed up to greet her, jumping up so his paws rested on her hips.

"Hey, boy, you been looking after the place." She gave him a big, long scratch behind his ears.

"About time you got home."

She looked up and smiled at Blaise walking toward her.

"Blaise." She rushed to him, and embraced his body, glad that he opened his arms to receive her. He felt good in her arms. Against her. She nestled into the base of his neck for a moment, enjoying how they reconnected too easily despite all that had been forcing them apart.

She had to make things clear to him.

So, she pulled away, and looked him square in the eyes. "Nothing happened. I want you to know that. And know that it is true."

He nodded.

She noticed he looked past her, so she turned, seeing Aaron limping over to his ute.

"I had to sort him out. He's finally got it that I choose you."

"He has?"

"Hey, I don't care if he hasn't. I don't mind if I have to kick his balls until he does gets it."

"Good, now what happened?"

"Nothing." She said the word with all her heart.

"That's not really what I want to hear."

She looked at him confused.

He smiled. "There was something else you told me, something else I'd rather hear you say.

She took a moment to realize what it was. "Oh…"

He raised his eyebrow, waiting.

"I love you." She grinned at him, wrapping her arms around his neck.

"I love you, too."

CHAPTER 10

Monday, December 23rd, 2019

Dusty was on the last round of the wheat crop. She'd taken time this morning to take a truckload to the silos, which meant now she could empty the combine straight into the bin on the truck, and all being well, take the last load to the silos tomorrow morning. Then she would clean the equipment, and she would then be officially finished before Christmas.

She planned to spend a few days relaxing, and more importantly, time with Blaise. She wanted him to stay in her life. She was sure of it now. Yet, it was still a big step, and she hadn't told him. It was getting difficult to keep it a secret, though. He had been going back to his rental in Wilkton in the evenings, so she hadn't seen a lot of him.

Things had settled between them after the trip with Aaron to Melbourne. She was glad that Blaise trusted and believed what she told him. It was the truth, after all.

One thing niggled at her—Blaise's Christmas present. Dusty wasn't big on gifts, but this year being their first Christmas together meant that she wanted to make an effort. She'd had an idea, but with each round of the paddock, she doubted herself.

Would the gift be enough?

Was it really a gift?

It was what Blaise wanted, and she was ready to give it to him.

The biggest issue was that she was simply running out of time, and she didn't have time to go to the local shops.

She turned the combine for the final time and finished the last of the crops for this year.

Done.

Satisfaction welled inside of her. She hadn't thought she'd manage to finish before Christmas. Relief washed over her while a tear slipped down her cheek. Another year nearly over, and the hard work was paying off.

Staying focussed, she drove to the truck and emptied the last load from the combine. It had been a difficult week, but now, as she finished, she needed to turn her attention to Blaise and their future together.

CHAPTER 11

Tuesday, December 24th, 2019 – Christmas Eve

Blaise couldn't believe that he managed to keep Claire's secret of moving out. During the last few days, they had made trip after trip into Wilkton to drop off the things she wanted to have with her. It was made a lot easier with Dusty hell-bent on finishing the harvest.

She had, yesterday. This morning she was taking the last truckload to the silos. She looked exhausted but happy that she'd done it.

Now, he was strolling along the eucalyptus trees around the fence line on the side paddock next to the house, looking for ideas for a gift for Dusty. He had a few ideas, and with Claire cooking up desserts after desserts in the house, he had a bit of time to himself.

He'd closed the books for the holiday season, and it felt good to be looking forward to Christmas with Dusty, spending more time with her, and seeing where that would lead them as a couple.

Blaise spied something that he thought would help make the perfect gift for Dusty. Bending down, he picked it up. He needed to add a few things, and he knew just what to do.

With Ted and Molly racing around him as he walked across the paddock back to the house, he headed back inside. Dusty had promised she would be back before dinner tonight. He was very much looking forward to that actually happening. Things seemed to take longer on the farm, so he'd already decided that if she were late, he wouldn't hold it against her.

First things first, he needed to finish her gift.

DUSTY HAD BEEN true to her word. She was proud of her efforts to get the harvest finished, the grain delivered, and the machinery cleaned and back in the shed for another year. It was satisfying.

Showered, in clean jeans and shirt, she sat at the table with Blaise and her mom, eating a light meal of chops and mashed potatoes with carrots and beans. Tomorrow she planned to overeat and enjoy her mom's cooking, then chill with Blaise.

On Boxing Day, she'd agreed to go with him to visit his parents. Spend a few days there. They were starting to do more things which showed they were a couple. The fear that had previously fluttered in her belly about this was gone. She was confident in her decision. And what she was going to announce to Blaise tonight.

Her mom was coming with them, and she was going to stay with her sister, Jody. Jody had decided to stay in Adelaide with her boyfriend on Christmas Day, much to her mom's disappointment. So, she had decided to invite herself to stay with Jody.

"At this rate, I won't be hungry tomorrow," said Blaise as he finished his meal. "No dessert for me."

"Are you sure?" asked Dusty.

Blaise always had dessert.

"Yep." He leaned back and patted his stomach.

"I've made an apple crumble pie," said Claire.

"A small piece then," said Blaise.

"That's more like you." Dusty smiled. To think she was nearly going to be too scared to have a future with him, and that she'd been running the risk of losing him. But not now.

"Before dessert, I have an announcement," said Claire.

Blaise looked a little sly.

"What?" asked Dusty. She had a sneaky suspicion they had both been up to something.

"I'm moving out."

"No." Dusty's mouth dropped open. "You can't. This is your home. You don't have anywhere to go."

"I do. I had a little nest egg of my own, and I've now got a room in the retirement home at Wilkton." Claire looked at her daughter. "You don't need me around now. You're going to start your own family."

"I can do that with you still living here."

"Maybe, but you two need your space to get adjusted to each other."

"When did this all happen?" She turned to Blaise. "Did you enable her?"

"I had no choice."

Dusty rolled her eyes. "Sure, you didn't."

"It's done, Dusty. And you will live here."

Dusty nodded. "This might just put a dampener on my gift to you, Blaise."

"Not possible." He grinned at her.

She put her hand on his arm. "I've made a decision." She looked directly into his eyes, seeing a flash of worry. "I want you to move in with me."

Blaise jumped up and fist punched the air in his excitement.

"About time," said Claire.

Blaise leaned down and planted a long kiss on Dusty's lips. "No dampener at all, and it's the best gift you could ever give me."

Dusty breathed a sigh of relief. "Good."

"Since we're giving out gifts," said Blaise. He slipped out of the kitchen and came back holding a small white gift box. "Merry Christmas, Dusty." He handed her the gift.

Her heart skipped as she took the small box, undid the golden bow, and lifted the lid. She smiled. Inside was a double gum nut, sprayed golden, with twisted wire around the top to form a loop so it could be hung on the tree.

"You listened to me," she spoke softly.

"Of course." He grinned at her.

"This will be the perfect addition to the Christmas tree." She looked at him, kissed him, feeling his heart joining with hers.

"The first of many." His eyes glowed with hope.

"Yes, the first of many," she answered him back with a certainty she never knew she had.

"Does this mean I can tell my friends over our coffee catch-up next week that you're both engaged?" asked Claire.

"Mom, you're—"

"Fine with me," Blaise interrupted. "Dusty? Will you marry me?"

Dusty giggled. Paused. Looked into his eyes again and felt herself melting with him. It was natural with him. A bit rocky at times, but hell, she never took the easy, smooth road. His look fueled a fire of passion within her.

There was only one answer to speak.

"Yes."

Dusty and Blaise relaxed together, the two of them on the couch listening to carols play from the stereo.

Dusty sighed happily. This was the content feeling she'd been hoping for with the crops safely reaped and delivered, and now spending time with Blaise. It had been a long job, but a job well done. She was exhausted, and her body ached. But it didn't matter. The feeling of love with Blaise and the satisfaction of a job well done more than made up for it.

She nestled into him, holding him close, enjoying the flicker of the Christmas lights in the room. Her gift from Blaise, a double gum nut, catching her eye and causing her to smile.

"You do know I'm missing the ring on my finger," she teased.

"You do know I wasn't at all planning to propose to you tonight. I didn't want to rush you."

"I've been a bit cautious."

"We're on track together now." He squeezed her tight.

"We are." She didn't care about the ring so much because everything felt right to her. That was what really mattered.

Dusty realized it was just past midnight.

"Merry Christmas." She kissed Blaise on the cheek. His skin soft, hot, and delightful to touch with her lips.

"Merry Christmas."

It felt great to have this time together, but it was so much more.

An engagement.

A promise.

There was a future together.

And she didn't need to worry otherwise.

"The first of many together."

"I look forward to every one of them with you."

Enjoy more rural romances
By Lilliana Rose
The Royal Show Affair
A Farmer's Christmas
Best in Show
A Country Christmas

Like urban paranormal romance?
Check out these books by Lilliana Rose
Protector Wolf Shifter Series
Bk1: Shadow Wolf
Bk2: Marked Wolf
Bk3: Rogue Wolf
Dragon Bond
Dragon Reborn
Witch Moon Series
Bk1: Dark Moon Secrets

ACKNOWLEDGMENTS

Thank you Kaylene for editing and always having time to offer support and advice.

Thanks to my sisters for their support of their crazy sister who is a writer, and my toddler boy for being well-behaved so I can still have time to write and nurture my soul.

Thanks to my dog Kimba, for reminding me when it's time to eat and to go to bed, and for simply just lying there next to me or at my feet, being that extra life in the room, so the writing journey isn't so lonely.

ABOUT THE AUTHOR

Lilliana Rose writes romance in the subgenres of contemporary, paranormal, and rural. She enjoys helping characters overcome problems, or issues, and the misunderstandings that often plague relationships, to help them fall in love. Whether it city heels being replaced with country work boots, or some magic beyond this world, each story shows how love can prevail. She has over fifteen years' experience in various education systems as a teacher, a skip and a jump from starting out in genetics research. It is all helpful for inspiring her writing. She has poetry, middle grade, picture book, novellas and novels published under various pen names.

Check out more of her work at www.lillianarose.com.

Connect with Lilliana Rose on social media.

9 780648 764076